# A TIME BEFORE ME

# A TIME BEFORE ME

*Michael Holloway Perronne*

iUniverse, Inc.
New York  Lincoln  Shanghai

# A TIME BEFORE ME

iUniverse books may be ordered through booksellers or by contacting:

iUniverse
2021 Pine Lake Road, Suite 100
Lincoln, NE 68512
www.iuniverse.com
1-800-Authors (1-800-288-4677)

ISBN: 0-595-33756-2

Printed in the United States of America

# *Prologue*

Ever notice how life gives you the answers to the big questions about a day late? That's exactly how I felt sitting in front of the apartment of the boy I loved in defeat. I looked at the bouquet of flowers that I had brought with me. They were already wilting in the oppressive New Orleans heat. They looked like I felt.

Miss Althea, the black drag queen who lived next door to him, walked up carrying three grocery bags from Schwegmann's stuffed to their brims. She wore a knee length yellow sundress, black sandals, and her "church" wig, the shoulder length red one with the curls. She eyed me curiously as she walked up the steps to her apartment.

"Baby, whatcha doin' sweatin' down there with them flowers next to ya?" she asked.

I debated on how much to tell her. There seemed to be three major forms of communication in New Orleans—telephone, telegraph, and teleMissAlthea. Anything you told her you could be sure everyone in the French Quarter would know by morning. They would be discussing it as they drank their chicory coffee, spreading the latest gossip, or *bizness*, in the neighborhood.

"I had just decided to stop by and see if he was home," I said.

Miss Althea took another look down at the flowers and then back up at me. She seemed on the verge of dropping her groceries and spilling them all over Rue Burgundy. However, she sensed that there was a story here, and she wasn't going anywhere.

"Baby, ain't you done heard?"

"Heard what?" I asked.

"That boy done gone. I saw him dis mornin' leaving with his suitcase by his side. He say he was goin' to his auntie's in Shreveport."

"Shreveport!" I exclaimed, standing up and dropping the flowers next to me.

"I'm sho surprised ya didn't know!" Miss Althea said.

She had a look on her face that said she was proud of the fact of being the first one to spread some fresh gossip.

I felt my heart sink into the pit of my stomach when I realized that I was too late, and that my own stupidity had gotten me to this point. Maybe I had just gotten exactly what I deserved.

By now you're probably wondering what the hell I'm talking about. I should go back to the beginning, or at least what I would consider the beginning.

It was the day that Billy Harris kissed me.

# CHAPTER 1

❀

It was 1990. The world wondered where society would take us in the new decade, and most importantly Madonna taught us how to vogue. It was her video for the song I was watching when my mother, Martha, came into the living room. She wore a pink, fuzzy robe and had those orange sponge curlers in her hair that I always found so funny. She had one hand on her hip and rolled her eyes. I knew that I must have screwed something up.

"Mason, when are you going to pick up those pecans? I have to start baking tonight for Thanksgiving, you know," she said, none too pleased.

I didn't look forward to standing in the bitter cold and shuffling through leaves in the search for pecans. It was especially cold for fall in Mississippi. The temperatures were dipping down in the twenties. I was warm and cozy, curled up in one of my mother's knit blankets on our black vinyl couch.

"Why can't Cherie help?" I begged.

I knew a Madonna marathon would be coming on VH1 later.

"Cherie has to prepare for the talent segment of the pageant," she answered, referring to my sister who was competing in the local Miss Peanut pageant. "Now get your ass out there and get me some pecans. I'm not telling you again."

And with that she left the living room.

I reluctantly put my shoes on, grabbed my winter coat, and headed down the hallway. On the way out, I caught a glimpse of Cherie putting on lip-gloss and admiring herself in the bathroom mirror. Preparing for a talent contest, my ass. She was busy making herself beautiful for her high school quarterback boyfriend, Houston. Looking back on it, I agree Houston was hot at the time. He stood over six feet tall to Cherie's five foot three, and he had dark brown hair and light blue eyes. Every girl, and probably some guys, in Andrew Springs were in love with him, and my beauty queen sister landed him.

As I headed outside into the cold, I wondered why I had to do all the shit work. I grabbed a rusty bucket that my mom kept out by the back steps just for this purpose and headed out to a grove of pecan trees just behind our house up on a hill overlooking the main drag in town, Peanut Boulevard.

Andrew Springs, named after the Andrews family that owned the local peanut processing plant, was a small town of just over ten thousand. About the most exciting thing that ever happened in Andrew Springs was when a new fast food place opened. That year it was Burger King on Peanut Boulevard. The local teenagers would drive their cars around and around the Burger King parking lot on Friday nights as a form of entertainment. Okay, I admit it. I had been around the Burger King block a few times myself, but the whole time I remember wondering if this was all there was in life. I sure prayed it wasn't.

I was a junior at Andrew Springs High and an okay student. I rarely made the honor roll but never came close to failing. The only thing I did do well was playing the sax in the high school band. I had come in third in a recent state competition. My father, Elvis, yes, he was named after the King, did his best to act proud. Although, I knew deep down he wished I were more like Houston.

When I made it to the top of the hill, I dropped the bucket beside me and sighed. I dreaded the idea of sifting through all of the leaves on the ground for the most perfect pecans, since they were the only ones my mother would accept. I bent down and started sorting through the dry, crackling leaves.

I glanced down the hill and saw the small brick house that belonged to one of my best friends, Billy Harris. His family had moved into the neighborhood when I was in the seventh grade. The first time I saw Billy I realized that I had feelings for boys that were just a little more than friendship. He was taller than me. He reached almost six feet by the time he was fourteen. His light blonde hair and light blue eyes were much more striking than my mousy brown hair and eyes. His smile was what got me in trouble though. Where I had to wear braces for four long years, Billy had a perfect, gleaming white smile. Because of that smile he seemed to be able to get along with everyone from the school nerds to the athletes. He had a way about him that always put everyone at ease, except my other best friend, Sylvia.

Sylvia had always lived three doors down from me. She always preferred wearing jeans instead of a dress, and she usually wore a baseball cap over her strawberry blonde hair. We had been friends as far back as I could remember, and we both shared a love of Madonna. She had secretly bought a copy of the

"Justify My Love" video on a family trip to Tupelo. We must have watched it a thousand times. She probably knew me better than anyone else.

Before Billy moved to town, it was usually just Sylvia and me hanging out. But once he moved in, I started wanting to spend a lot of time with him, too. I especially liked it when we were alone. I could just listen to him talk for hours while we sat in his bedroom eating Doritos. He spoke of how one day he'd move to the big city.

"The world is so big, Mason," he often told me. "How could you not want to see as much of it as you can?"

Sometimes the three of us would do things together, like go to the movies or hang out in the arcade outside of Wal-Mart. Sylvia was entirely immune to Billy's charms, and I always noticed that she seemed to act a little strangely when it was the three of us together. She was quieter and often seemed very distant.

I began to shiver as I looked down at my bucket. It was only a fourth of the way full of pecans and definitely not enough for my Mom's pies.

"Shit!" I muttered under my breath. I realized I should have done this earlier in the day. The sun was at least partly out then.

"Hey, Mace!" I heard Billy call out from behind me.

I turned around to find Billy breathing hard and walking over towards me rolling his bike by his side. He was dressed only in a pair of jeans and a light pullover.

"Man, I love riding my bike in this kind of weather. The cold air really gets ya going!" he said.

He raised his shirt to wipe some of the sweat off his face.

I felt my heart go into double time as I caught a peek of the happy trail of hair that led down to his crotch. What I would have done to lick the sweat off of that stomach!

"Aren't you cold?" I asked, wrapping my arms around myself.

"Cold is a state of mind, Mason," he said, as if that should make sense. "What are you doing later tonight?"

"I dunno. Why?"

*Please invite me over, I wanted to say!*

"My parents left yesterday on an overnight trip. I got the place all to myself, and…" he said. He leaned in closer and his voice turned into a half-whisper, "I was able to score a six pack of beer."

The only time I had ever drunk a beer was at my cousin Sarah's backyard wedding. My head spun, I made a fool of myself dancing to a Cyndi Lauper song, and then I vomited the rest of the night while my aunt stood by the toilet shaking her head and wiping my face.

"Sounds like a blast," I said.

"Great. Why don't you come over around seven-thirty? Cool?"

"Cool," I said.

"See ya," he said.

He hopped on his bike and took off.

I stood there for a moment and watched him ride off. I looked at my watch and saw it was four thirty. I knew my mom wouldn't let me go anywhere until she had enough pecans. All of a sudden, I felt quite motivated.

"You in a rush or something?" my father asked.

He noticed that I was practically gulping down my food.

"Hungry, I guess," I replied, looking up at the clock. It was seven-fifteen.

My father reached over and slapped me on my back and laughed.

"Growing boy," he said.

"It's not good to eat so fast," my mother said sharply.

My parents insisted that the whole family always eat dinner together. It was not something that I particularly looked forward to enduring. I never felt like I had anything to say to any of them. Cherie just spent the whole time talking about pageants, Houston, or her cheerleading squad. I usually just sat in silence waiting for the time to go by so I could go watch MTV. Ever since my parents had given me a television for my bedroom, I never saw much of a reason to leave my room if I was home.

"Is that all you're having?" Mom asked Cherie, who barely touched her meatloaf.

It seemed funny to me that I always ate too much, and Cherie didn't eat enough.

"If I'm going to fit in that new dress for the pageant I have to watch what I eat, Mother," Cherie answered.

"Oh, you girls. You shouldn't be starving yourselves," Mom said.

She reached over for the bowl of mashed potatoes and another large helping.

"May I be excused?" I asked.

*Please let me go before I scream!*

"Why? You got a hot date?" Dad cracked.

"Uh, no," I said. "I was just going to go hang out at Billy's."

Then I had one of those moments where I just wanted to reach over and slap someone up side the head when Cherie said, "You go over there an awful lot."

"It's better than sitting around here listening to you talk about how great you think you are," I snapped back.

"You're just jealous because I was voted most popular, and you would have never gotten one vote in a million years!" she said.

She tossed back her mane of shoulder length red hair. I could have ripped it out strand by strand with a smile on my face.

"Kids!" Mom said. She slammed her fist on the table. "You're giving me a headache. Why do you have to be so mean to each other?"

"He started it!" Cherie said.

Suddenly, she tore into her meatloaf with her fork.

"Whatever, Miss Priss!" I said.

"Mason, go!" Mom said. "It's better than listening to the two of you argue right now."

"Thank you," I said.

I got up from the table.

"Who's got the TV Guide?" Dad asked, looking around the room.

Walking along the quiet pine tree lined street to Billy's, I could feel the butterflies in my stomach going into overdrive. That always happened if I knew I would be spending time with him alone. Looking back on it, I guess you could say I was in love with him, or at least what I thought of as being "in love." When I started high school, my parents began to notice my lack of interest in girls. I never talked about them and rarely went on any dates. One time they even had a conversation in front of me, about me, that maybe I was too shy or a late bloomer. Cherie had begun dating practically the moment she left the womb. Comparing me to her, they couldn't seem to figure out what was the problem. At one point, they began to think maybe something was going on between Sylvia and me. They eventually lost hope in that hook-up.

In Andrew Springs, if you aren't married by the time you're twenty, people begin to start wondering what's wrong with you. I went on a couple of dates with some girls from school to try and please my parents. The whole time I thought about how much happier I would be if I were out with my date's hot basketball-playing brother.

I had often wondered if Billy might have the same type of feelings that I did about other boys, but then I wondered if it was just wishful thinking. Billy attracted a lot of girls. They always seemed to flock to him. Sometimes he would take them out, but he never mentioned doing anything physical with them. He never really seemed to be lusting after them like so many of the guys at school. But he had that type of winning personality where no one seemed to even question his dating habits.

After I knocked on the door, it took only a few moments before he opened it. He was wearing a white T-shirt, that was just a little too tight, and he already had a beer in his hand.

"Hey, just in time for the party, my man!" he said.

He opened the door wide and let me in.

It was warm and toasty inside. The smell of pepperoni pizza drifted through the air.

"I had some pizza delivered. Want some?" he offered.

He slugged down the last of the beer.

"Nah. Thanks. I just ate."

His parents had just been gone for a day and already the living room was a mess. Empty bowls, plates, glasses, and magazines were all around the room. The stereo was blasting Martika's song "Toy Soldiers". He collapsed on the couch, reached over, and grabbed another beer off the coffee table.

"Have one," he said, motioning to them.

I sat down next to him and took a beer, hesitating at first when I remembered my cousin's wedding.

"Go on. Loosen up," he said.

He opened the can and drank a gulp.

"Damn, must be nice to have the place to yourself. Never happens to me," I said.

I popped the top on my beer.

"Yeah, it's so fucking freeing," he said.

He slipped his hand into his jeans and scratched his balls, which he did sometimes if we were alone. An odd habit, I thought, but also one that excited me.

"They'll be back for Thanksgiving, right?" I asked.

"Yeah, unfortunately. Who gives a crap about some turkey?" he said softly.

I could tell the alcohol had already begun to take its effect on him. I braced myself and took a sip, trying hard not to make a face. I had always thought beer tasted like crap. Once again, I was proven right.

"Man, can you believe we're going to be seniors next year?" he said, his eyes drifting off.

"Yeah, I can't wait to get outta there."

"Have you thought about what you want to do?" he asked, with an unusually serious tone to his voice.

"Hell, I don't know," I said. I ran my finger over the rim of the beer can. "Maybe go to the junior college for a while. Can you believe Dad said he would try and get me a job at the peanut plant?"

Billy burst out laughing.

"No shit!" he exclaimed. "The cycle continues, huh?"

"Huh?"

"Didn't your grandpa work there, too?" he asked.

"Yeah."

"Looks like your dad wants you to have the same life as him," Billy said.

My mind fast-forwarded twenty years later to me with a beer gut, a dead-end job, and a broken down Ford pick-up.

"Screw that," I said.

"Parents should want better for their kids," he began. "But, I think some of them want to see their kids live the same exact life they did so that way they won't feel like they missed out on anything themselves."

"And what do you want to do?"

He contemplated for a moment and ran his fingers through his hair.

"To get the fuck out of Mississippi," he said finally.

I laughed.

"You're always talking about that. To go where?"

"Shit, I don't know. Somewhere. If someone wants to stay here that's fine for them, but some people want to do other things with their lives, too. There is nothing wrong with that. My parents don't even look at it like it's an option. They'd probably just be happy with me staying here, getting married, knocking the girl up, and working at the gas station."

The beer was beginning to hit me. I felt a warm feeling coarse through my veins.

"Yeah. Who wants to do that?" I said.

Billy burst out laughing.

"Yeah, who wants to marry some girl and get her pregnant," he said, with an eyebrow cocked. "Would you want that, Mace?"

I paused for a moment, and I wondered what he could be trying to get at. It couldn't possibly be what I thought he might be trying to say.

"I dunno…" I said, my voice trailing off.

"Yeah, I just bet," he said.

He eyed me with a wicked look.

"What does that mean?"

"I guess you could say that I just don't see you as the marrying type."

He reached for another beer, opened it, and took a long sip.

"Well, what about you? I see you hanging out with all of these girls all of the time, but you never seem to do much about it," I said, getting a little defensive and taking a gulp of my own beer.

"Hey, hey, hey," he said.

He slid over on the sofa next to me. I could feel my heart rate increase what seemed like ten times, and I hoped he wouldn't notice the huge erection that had popped up in my pants.

"I'm just making conversation," he said. "Just making an observation that you never, ever talk about girls, or seem much interested in them at all."

"I don't know. I'm just shy, I guess," I mumbled.

"Ah, come on, Mace," he said.

He slowly wrapped one of his arms around me.

I swallowed hard. I looked down and noticed that my hands were slightly shaking.

"How long have we known each other?" he asked.

"Since seventh grade. You know that," I replied.

"That's a long time," he said.

I turned and looked into his eyes and saw that glassy, hazy look come over his face that I had come to recognize as the look of someone who was really drunk.

"Yeah?" I said.

"Have you even so much as kissed a girl?" he asked.

"Have you?" I countered.

He just started laughing.

"What do you think?" he asked.

"I dunno…"

He then made a move that I swear made my heart stop for a brief second. With his hand he lifted up my chin so that our eyes met. I felt at that moment I could get lost forever just staring into his light blue eyes. Up until that point, it was the most powerful moment that I had ever felt.

"What if I kissed you?" he asked.

"Huh?" I said.

My hands begin to shake even more.

"Don't pretend like you didn't hear me," he said.

All of a sudden, he wrapped his other arm around me and pulled me close.

"I don't feel you pulling away," he mumbled in my ear.

His mouth made its way to mine, and it's true that I didn't pull away. In fact, I didn't do anything but sit there frozen, too scared or too excited to make a move. At first he started kissing me softly with gentle pecks, but then I felt his tongue part my lips, and he began to kiss me passionately.

"Billy…" I struggled to say when he paused to take a breath.

"Shhh," he said, his warm breath smelled strongly of beer. "Just be quiet, okay?"

He leaned me back on the couch, climbed on top of me, and continued kissing me. After a while, I began to kiss back, and I wrapped my arms around his body. I slipped my hands underneath his t-shirt and ran my hands over the soft, smooth skin I had wanted to touch for so long. I held him as tight as I could. At that moment I thought right there that I knew what heaven must feel like. There was no other place I could possibly want to be than right there with the boy that I had thought of on so many lonely nights lying on top of me, his weight pressing down on me, feeling his hard-on against my leg.

He began to start moving down and kissing my neck.

"Billy, I…" I whispered softly.

He said nothing but rested his head on my chest.

I looked down at the top of his head and wrapped my arms around him even tighter.

"How did you know I felt this way, Billy?" I asked softly. "I've always wanted my first kiss to be with you."

I waited for a response but heard nothing. I decided that if I had started telling him how I felt that I might as well continue. To hell with it! I would just let it all out.

"The reason I never asked any girls out is because you're the one I want. You've always been the one that I wanted since the first day you rode your bike over to my house when we were in the seventh grade. You were the one that I wanted, Billy."

Still no response.

"Billy?"

And then I heard it. He began to snore softly, and I knew he was asleep. Actually, he had more like passed out, and I realized that he hadn't heard so much as a word of what I had said while I poured my heart out to him. He had slept through my entire confession.

After a couple of hours, I began to realize that he wasn't going to wake up any time soon. I wasn't sure what to do with him lying on top of me, still snoring softly. For a while, I just enjoyed it knowing that we were in this intimate position, but then I remembered my mother would be expecting me home sometime soon. She was the type who would wait up if one of her children were still out and about.

So as gently as I could, I scooted out from under Billy and let his body fall on the couch. I was scared that I was going to wake him. If I did, what would I say? What would he say about what had just happened? I was still trying to process it in my own mind. But he didn't so much as stir. His body fell on the couch like a dead weight.

I stood there for a moment and just stared at him. He looked so handsome and sweet lying there sleeping. I reached down on the floor by the couch and picked up a small quilt and covered him up with it, and then I bent down and placed a small kiss on his forehead.

On the walk home, I kept going over and over in my head what had happened that night. I kept wondering what Billy say when we saw each other next.

# CHAPTER 2

It was a little after ten in the morning. I sat in the living room and watched Oprah talk to people who had collectively lost over two thousand pounds. The phone rang, and something told me it was him. When my mom told me Billy was on the phone, I felt my heart rate go into overdrive again. This was it. It was the moment of truth.

"Man, I am so hung over," Billy said.

"Yeah, I felt a little like crap this morning when I got up," I said.

I wondered when he would mention what happened last night. I mean we did *make out*.

"It was a wild night, huh?" I asked, hoping he would take the bait.

"Yeah, I guess so," he replied. "Oh, crap!"

"What?"

"Gotta go. My parents just pulled up. I got to straighten up the living room, pronto. I'll call you later," he said, abruptly hanging up on me.

I sat there for a few moments with the receiver still next to my ear kind of in shock that he didn't mention what we did the previous night.

*At all!*

What did this mean?

I proceeded to stare at Oprah wipe the tears from her eyes as she described her own battle with weight loss. My mind raced trying to come to a conclusion about the situation.

Mother walked into the living room wiping her hands on a dishrag and shaking her head in disapproval.

"So are you going to spend your whole Thanksgiving vacation rotting in front of the television?" she asked.

I sighed and prayed that she didn't want me to go pick more pecans for those damn pies.

"I'm just chilling out!" I protested.

"Chilling out?" my mother said. "Is that some new lingo you kids have come up with so that you don't have to use proper English?"

I could tell I was in a no-win situation. The thing my mother hated more than anything else was to see others doing nothing while she was busy.

"The least you can do is vacuum the house for me. Your Aunt Savannah will be here soon."

That brought a small smile to my face. My Aunt Savannah was always the life of any family gathering. She lived in what my mother referred to as "Sin City", New Orleans. Even though we lived only a five-hour drive from New Orleans, I had never been there. I loved hearing Aunt Savannah's stories about what it was like living in the Quarter. Often times when she would visit the two of us would sit on the back porch in the swing, me with my legs crossed and her filing her nails. She would tell me about the Mardi Gras balls she would attend, the Jazz Fest, and all of the colorful people that lived in her neighborhood.

When she was just a teen, Aunt Savannah moved to New Orleans for reasons that were never really explained to me, and somehow I sensed that I was not supposed to ask. All that I did know was that Savannah married at one point, and she inherited some money with which she used to buy a theater in the French Quarter where all the performers were female impersonators, or as she called them, drag queens. She hosted the shows, and, apparently, she was sort of famous around town. She used to tell me all of the time about parties and dinners where she would hobnob with the New Orleans elite and celebrities that were in town visiting. She even got me an autograph from Johnny Depp, who she met at a party, because she knew *21 Jump Street* had been one of my favorite shows.

Aunt Savannah was a sight to behold with her bright blonde hair. "The best a bottle can give you," she often said. She always wore huge earrings, her trademark. And even though she was now in her mid-forties, she still wore skirts that were so short that everyone's head in Andrew Springs would turn when she would visit. She was also fond of showing off her cleavage, of which she certainly had no shortage.

Even though I was always sure of the fact that she and my mother loved each other, it amazed me that they could actually be sisters. Where Aunt Savannah was so flamboyant, my mother was always dressed very plainly, with her graying mousy brown hair pulled back in a bun. Where Aunt Savannah was always laughing, my mother rarely cracked a smile.

When she would visit, my mother always seemed exasperated where her sister was concerned. She seemed embarrassed about how she dressed and what she did for a living. "Men parading in women's clothes! It's Satan on stage," she often said if I brought up Aunt Savannah's theater.

Aunt Savannah, too, often seemed to not understand my mother. Yet she always visited a few times a year. She actually seemed to visit more after both of my grandparents died.

Only once did I discover that there might actually be a bond between my mother and aunt that I never realized before. It was during one of my aunt's visits at Christmas. Late one night I got up to get a drink of water, and I heard voices from the living room. I was surprised since I realized one of them was my mother's voice. She was always in bed by ten, but it was well past two.

I tiptoed towards the living room to hear better. From a distance I saw my mother cradling my aunt's head in her lap. My aunt cried while my mother gently patted her head.

"Let it out, honey. Let it out," she said.

I stood there for a moment and watched. I had never seen such tenderness take place between them.

"She was so beautiful, Sissy," my aunt said, between sobs. "I see that pretty little precious face ever night before I go to bed. Every night, I swear."

"I know, honey. I know," my mother said, wiping one of my aunt's tears away.

I quietly made my way back to my room, and the next morning the two of them seemed to be back to normal. My mom even asked my aunt if she was "really going to wear that blouse to Christmas dinner." Only later did I realize what they were talking about that night.

So I began to help my mother around the house as she prepared for the holiday. My father still had to work that day, and Cherie had driven to the Metro Center Mall in Jackson with some friends of hers to do some advance Christmas shopping. How she always seemed to get out of doing anything always perplexed me.

Later that afternoon, my mother had decided I could have a break. Sylvia stopped by and dragged me with her to the Kroger's uptown. Her mother sent her to buy some last minute Thanksgiving supplies. Like a nut, I agreed to go, even though I knew how packed a supermarket would be the day before a holiday.

On the way there, we blasted her Samantha Fox cassette and sung along to "Naughty Girls Need Love Too". Sylvia seemed in a particularly good mood.

"So is it true what I heard?" I asked, as we neared the supermarket.

"Is what true?"

"Oh, come on. About you and Ryan Shoemaker?"

She blushed slightly.

"I heard he has a big crush on you," I said.

"And who did you hear that from?"

"Billy."

She turned down the music and wheeled into the parking lot.

"What does Billy know anyway?" she said.

Her good mood seemed to evaporate.

"He had just heard," I answered, confused at her quick change in attitude.

"I stopped by to see you last night," she said. She parked her mother's 1985 Oldsmobile that was as long and wide as a yacht. "Your mom said you were over at Billy's."

"Yeah, we were hanging out."

"Just the two of you?"

"Yeah, why?"

"Just curious," she said.

She hopped out of the car and slammed the door behind her.

I got out and followed her. I didn't know what it was about Billy that got under her skin so much, and then my mind wandered back to what Billy and I had done the night before. My heart began to beat faster at the thought of it, and I wondered if there was any sort of a chance of a repeat.

"Little Bit, go get Auntie some ice for her cocktail," Aunt Savannah said.

She handed me her glass that was half full of vodka.

As far back as I could remember, her nickname for me had been Little Bit. The story behind it was that when I was around three she asked me, "So you love your Aunt Savannah, sweetie?"

I shrugged my shoulders and answered, "Little bit."

I went into the kitchen and put more ice in the glass, and headed back into the dining room. Aunt Savannah was holding court at the table, as we had our traditional pre-Thanksgiving dinner of Popeye's Fried Chicken.

"So where's that strapping hunk of a boyfriend of yours, sweetie?" she said, turning to Cherie.

"He's going to stop by tomorrow afternoon."

Cherie tossed back her hair and batted her eyes, pleased with herself that she dated the school stud.

"Well, I hope to see him," Savannah said, winking.

"Savannah!" Mother exclaimed.

"Oh, Sissy! Don't tell me you haven't noticed that boy's fine butt?" Savannah said.

She took a sip of her traditional cocktail of vodka mixed with a splash of club soda and a wedge of lime.

"He's a high school boy!" mother said.

"I know that, but that doesn't mean he's not cute, huh, girl?" Savannah said, elbowing Cherie.

Cherie just giggled.

My father sighed as he stared across the room at the evening news on the television. He rarely said much, especially if Aunt Savannah was around.

"Still…" mother muttered.

"And how have you been, Elvis?" Savannah called across the table, breaking my father's concentration.

"Huh?" he grunted.

He wasn't used to having someone speak to him at the table.

"Life treating you well?"

My father scratched his growing belly. His eyes drifted back to the television.

"Guess I can't complain," he answered.

Savannah turned back to my mother.

"You two should come to New Orleans for a vacation. It'd do you both good to get out of town for a few days," she said. Her voice turned to a half whisper. "Rekindle the old romance."

Mother blushed.

"We'll have to see. We're so busy with everything," she said,

"I want to visit sometime," I spoke up.

My mother raised a disapproving eyebrow.

"Oh, that'd be so much fun, Little Bit. I could show some of the fun things the city has to offer," Aunt Savannah said. She reached over and ruffled my hair, something she still did even though I was now sixteen.

"You have school to worry about," mother said.

"Really, Sissy! It won't hurt the boy to see something outside of this dusty town," Aunt Savannah said. She leaned over and said to me, "Don't you worry, Little Bit. I'll work on your mama."

There was a knock at the front door.

"I'll get it," I said.

I got up from the table and smiled at my aunt. I hoped that she would be able to convince my mother.

When I made it to the front door, I peeked out the window and saw that it was Billy. I was immediately filled with excitement and a little fear. Now maybe we could *finally* talk about everything that had happened the night before.

"Hey," I said.

"Hey," he said.

He ran his fingers through his blond hair and looked away.

"What's up?" I asked.

"Just thought I'd stop by. Kind of bored. My parents are driving me up a wall already," he said. He kicked at some dirt near the front step and ruined his previously pristine white, new sneakers. "Wanna go for a walk?"

I swallowed hard, and I felt the butterflies in my stomach go into overdrive.

"Yeah, sure," I said. "I'll be right back."

I went and told my mom, who for once said that Cherie could clear the table since she had gone to Jackson most of the day. I grabbed my jacket and rushed outside.

As we walked down the road past the other homes, where inside families were preparing for the holiday, we remained silent. Every now and then Billy would look up at the sky and its twinkling bright stars.

"I just wish my parents would ease up on me," he said, finally breaking the silence.

"Why what's going on?" I asked. Inside I thought that with everything in me all I wanted to do was to grab him and kiss him like I had the previous night.

"They got a progress report from school. I'm failing algebra," he said.

"That sucks."

"I mean, who gives a crap about what x plus y equals?"

"I dunno."

"I can't wait until graduation. I'm getting the hell out of here," he said.

I noticed that he was balling his hands up into fists at his sides.

"Yeah, right," I said laughing.

He stopped walking and turned to me with a look that bordered on angry.

"I am. First thing I'm getting the hell out," he said.

"Okay, okay," I said.

He wrapped his arms around himself as he began to shake slightly.

"It's getting cold. Let's go home."

So we turned around and started walking back, again in silence. The awkwardness between us was so thick, I swear, I could feel it as I breathed. As we made it back to my house, we stopped in front of my parent's driveway.

"Have a good Thanksgiving," I said.

I hoped to get a smile out of him.

"Yeah, yeah," he said. "You, too."

Billy started to walk towards his house, and I decided that if anyone was going to say anything it looked like it was going to be me.

"Hey, Billy!" I called after him.

He stopped and turned around.

"I just wanted to say…about…" I began.

"Oh, yeah, my mom said to tell your family Happy Thanksgiving for her," he said, cutting me off before I could say anything more.

"Oh, okay," I said.

"See ya later," he said.

Billy turned around and headed back to his house.

Shivering in the cold, I stood there for a moment and watched him walk away.

# CHAPTER 3

❀

Before I knew it, the holidays were over, and then the spring, and then the summer, and finally the next fall. All of a sudden, I found myself a high school senior with graduation fast approaching. Cherie, who was now a freshman in college, was preparing herself to take part in the Miss Mississippi Pageant. Her boyfriend, Houston, was on the football team at Ole Miss. He hoped to go pro. My father followed Houston's football career closely. He was as proud of him as if he were his own son.

One day, on one of the rare occasions that I was alone with my father, he took me with him to a lumberyard in the next town. He was building a new work shed in the back and needed someone to help him load the wood on the truck. We drove most of the way in silence, which was often the case. My father felt like someone that I should know, but often felt like a distant stranger.

Most of what I did know about him I learned from other people. His mother had died of cancer when he was less than three. My grandfather, who apparently spent most of his time at a local bar, was left to raise him. He never talked about his childhood. Most of what I knew about it came from my great-grandmother, who we called Grams. She had obviously been more of a parent to him than his father. His father usually drank away each week's pay; so she was the one that fed and clothed him.

Before she died, when I was around ten, she would come and stay with us for a month every summer from her home in Greenville. Some summer afternoons if it was just too hot to play outside, I would sit on the floor next to her in the rocking chair. Every afternoon she would do the same thing. She would sit in the living room knitting sweaters, that she would eventually give away that year for Christmas and watch her soap operas, or what she called her "stories."

In between commercials, she would sometimes tell me tales about my father when he was a boy. Some were funny and were some sad. She told me about the time that he had a huge crush on a girl in the sixth grade and told Grams he was going to marry her some day. The little girl turned out to be my mother.

She also told me how one Christmas, when he was around eleven, they were flat broke, and my grandfather had been out of work for some time. My father had gone out in the woods and sawed down a small pine tree and brought it home. He had then made his own decorations out of paper and crayons. No matter what, he was determined that they were going to have Christmas.

After a few minutes of talking to me, her story would come back on the television, and she'd say something like, "Shhh…she goin' go and find out about him runnin' around on her."

Her funeral had also been the one and only time I had ever seen him cry.

My father cleared his throat, which brought my thoughts back to the present. He turned down the farm news, which was reporting the latest hog prices, on the radio.

"Son, I want to talk to you about something," he said.

I knew nothing good could be coming next. He never talked to me unless it was something I really didn't want to hear.

"Yeah?" I asked.

"You been thinking about what you're going to do once you get out of high school?"

I fidgeted in the truck seat.

"Yeah, I've thought about it some."

"And?"

"I don't know."

"Well," he began, "Now is the time to start thinking about it."

"Maybe I'll go to the junior college," I said, trying to come up with a quick answer.

"Well, ya know, son, me and your mom don't have much money. Cherie got that cheerleading scholarship, and that's how come she got to go to the college."

I looked out of the window at the endless forest of pine trees. It was a vast sea of green disrupted only by a two-lane highway.

I wasn't sure what he wanted me to say. If I couldn't go to college, what would I do? What was here for me, really?

"Well…" I said, for lack of a better response.

"Ya know, I could talk to Mr. Peterson at the peanut factory about getting you on. If you start now, you could maybe move up to something there after a while."

*No! Please, God, no! Anything but the peanut factory!*

"The peanut factory?" I said.

I felt my stomach tie up in knots.

"Well, you're gonna have to do something, and that's about as good of a job as any around here," he said.

He reached over and turned the radio back up. I could tell he was getting frustrated with me.

As we turned into the lumberyard, he said, "I'll tell you what, son. I'll talk to Mr. Peterson, and in the meantime, if you come up with something better, we'll talk about it."

I knew that was the end of the conversation. My feelings had been already dismissed. I had to come up with a plan of my own…and fast.

That afternoon I met Sylvia outside the Winn Dixie where she worked as a cashier. She had her hair pulled back in a haphazard ponytail, and her name tag was crooked on her employee vest. I watched as she dug into her rocky road ice cream, as if she hadn't eaten in a week.

"I can't believe that's what you're having for lunch," I told her. I shuddered as I realized that sounded like something my mother would have said.

"Hey, it's got calcium in it," she said in her defense.

She looked over and noticed that I hadn't even touched my ice cream sandwich. I would have normally inhaled about half of at that point.

"What's wrong with you?" she asked.

"My dad thinks I should go work at the peanut factory when I graduate high school."

She laughed so hard she began to snort. I thought rocky road might start coming out of her nose.

"It's not funny!" I said.

"I'm sorry," she said.

She tried to catch her breath.

"What am I going to do? I'd rather die than work there!"

"Don't be so dramatic, geez!" she said.

She polished off her ice cream and then picked up a napkin and daintily wiped her mouth as if she had just eaten a gourmet meal.

"I'm serious! I don't want to have my dad's life."

"Well, what do you want to do?"

I paused and thought about it again.

"I don't know. I don't have a clue," I said.

"Well, you know you don't want to work at the peanut factory, so you better come up with a plan to make sure it doesn't happen. What about college?"

I picked at the nuts on my sundae. I felt so sick that even the hot fudge wasn't tempting.

"Yeah, I want to go, but my dad says he has no money for it. Let's face it my grades aren't going to win me any scholarships."

Sylvia's eyes drifted off for a moment in deep thought.

"What are you thinking?" I asked.

"What about a band scholarship? The junior college gives them away."

"I'm not sure I'm good enough."

I barely practiced anymore, and I somehow managed to even get out of going to any of the away football games with the rest of the band.

"Well, better start practicing. I know they have tryouts every spring semester."

I drummed my fingers on the table in contemplation.

"Either that or you can be peanut inspector number thirteen," she said, getting up. "I gotta get back. People gotta check out their groceries."

And with that she left me there thinking that maybe this was an option.

I stayed late at school to practice my sax for the competition. If I was going to have any chance of winning a scholarship, I had a lot of practice to do, and I knew it. Over the past year my interest in playing had begun to wane, and my performance showed it. I couldn't even hit the high notes that I once played with ease. I made a vow to practice at least for an hour and a half, every single day, until the competition.

I wish I would've stayed later at school though. When I got home that afternoon, I was dumbfounded. Cherie and our father stood outside in the front yard, and he was screaming profanities at her. My father was always a man of few words, even the times he was angry, except on this occasion. I stopped in the middle of the yard, right by my mother's rose beds, not quite sure what to do.

Finally, my mother flew out the front door waving her hands in the air like a crazy woman.

"Elvis! The neighbors! Please!" she pleaded.

My father turned to Cherie, who was in tears, and pointed a finger at her.

"We worked our asses off, girl, to give you a better life, and this is how you repay us?"

"But Daddy…" Cherie sobbed.

"Not another word," my father said. He tried to get himself under control. "You want to mess up your life? I sure as hell can't stop you."

And with that he hopped in his pick-up truck and peeled out of the driveway.

I noticed nosy Ms. Henderson across the street peeking out of her window to see what all the commotion was about. I'm sure she was on the phone in a matter of seconds calling fellow neighbors.

Cherie ran to our mother and threw her arms around her.

"I'm sorry, Mama," she cried. "But it's what I have to do."

My mother patted her on the back as she held her, but her face was almost void of any emotion.

"Go on in, girl, and dry your tears. You have to pull yourself together," she said.

Cherie pulled back, and they both noticed me staring at them in confusion. I had never seen my sister look so genuinely frightened. I knew whatever happened was big.

"What's going on?" I asked.

Cherie looked at our mother not knowing what to say.

"Go on in," my mother said to her.

Reluctantly, Cherie went in with the screen door slamming behind her.

"Well?" I said.

Mother looked across the street, and caught a glimpse of Mrs. Henderson looking out at us through her curtains.

"Come inside," she told me.

We went in, and I followed her to the kitchen, where she poured herself a big cup of coffee. She sat down at the dining room table and smoothed back a few loose hairs on her head.

I sat down across from her and said," Whatever it is, it can't be that bad."

"Not according to your father," she said.

"Why was Dad so angry?"

"Cherie is going to lose her cheerleading scholarship, and she will have to drop out of the Miss Mississippi Pageant."

"Whoa! Why?"

I knew the two most important things in the world to my sister were cheering and pageants.

"She's pregnant," my mother said matter-of-factly, as she sipped her coffee. "She and Houston will be getting married. Obviously, she can't cheer then, and she can't be in the pageant."

"Pregnant?" I said.

My jaw practically dropped on the table.

The whole time growing up I felt like my parents looked to Cherie as the perfect one. She would never do anything such as get pregnant without the benefit of marriage. She was going to continue making the pageant circles, win tons of scholarships, and go on to a great, big, bright future.

"That's what I said," my mother said.

"What's going to happen now? What is Houston going to do?"

"Well, he's going to have to drop out of school. He can't support a wife and child while he is in school."

No more possible football career. Another one of my dad's dreams shot to hell.

"I can't believe this," I said.

My mother reached over, and grabbed my hand.

"Mason, I know that you and your sister have never exactly been close, and I don't agree with the way she has handled her life recently. But please be nice to her. She's going to need support now more than ever if she's going to really make a go of this. It's going to be tough."

I nodded, still in shock.

After school the next day, I met Billy at a park that was near our houses. He was there doing some sort of research project for his biology class. Neither one of us had brought up what happened on that Thanksgiving. It was as if it had never happened. My crush on Billy did not subside in the least; in fact, it was just as strong as ever. Not a day went by where I didn't fantasize about how his body felt that night, the taste of his kisses, or the soft snoring sound he made as his head lay on my chest. I prayed that the events of that night would end up repeating itself.

"How's it going?" I asked.

He stood in the small field behind the park picking flowers and carefully placing them in a paper bag. Spring was in full force as the wild flowers of red, yellow, and white were in abundant supply.

The oppressive Southern heat was also beginning to rear its ugly head. The air was so humid it felt like you could cut it with a knife.

"Stupid biology class...stupid botany project," he mumbled.

He leaned down to pick a small yellow flower, but then decided against it, so he just stepped on it.

I put my backpack on the ground and sat down.

Billy, seemed to give up, walked over, and sat down next to me. He took a bottle of water out of his book bag and began to drink. I noticed once again how his muscles seemed to be developing into those of a man's. His biceps were getting bigger and turning into a small bulge on his arms, and I could tell his chest was getting wider. All of this seemed to come to him with no effort on his part. I, on the other hand, still had the body of a skinny boy.

"Big news about your sister. Everybody in town is talking about it," Billy said, when he finished his water.

I rolled my eyes. You couldn't fart in Andrew Springs without everyone else knowing about it.

"Yeah, dad's pretty freaked out about the whole thing. Houston's family is pissed. But the wedding is still in two weeks," I said.

"Sounds like it'll be a happy occasion."

"Yeah, I'm sure the laughs will be rolling out," I said. "Did I tell you I'm trying out for the junior college band?"

"Really? No. Why?"

"Sylvia told me about it. If they like me enough, I could get a scholarship. Otherwise, what am I going to do? Go work with my dad?"

"I want to show you something," he said.

He looked around the park like he was about to reveal some top-secret information.

He opened up his backpack, took out a small booklet, and handed it to me. I saw that it was a bus schedule.

"What's this?" I asked.

"The future," he said grinning.

I looked down at it again.

"I still don't get it."

"It's a bus schedule."

"Yeah, and?"

He grunted in annoyance.

"The night of graduation I'm leaving for New York City," he said.

"Do what?!" I exclaimed.

"I saved money all last summer working with my uncle's construction company. Over a thousand dollars!"

"You're just going to up and go all the way to New York City? You've never even been there!"

"Not for much longer. The bus line is running a special on tickets. I already bought one, and I bought a book," he said.

He opened his backpack again and pulled out a book titled "A Newcomers Guide to the Big Apple."

"But why New York City?"

The thought made my mind spin.

"Mace, the Big Apple, the city that never sleeps! There can't be a better place in the whole world to go and start a brand new life, can it?"

"I just know you're not serious," I said, shaking my head. "You've never even been to a big city in your whole life."

"I'll figure it out when I get there. I'll have no other choice," he said confidently. "And I'm not even going to tell my parents beforehand."

"They're going to freak!"

Billy's mother was especially overprotective. She once freaked out when we came back from a school dance fifteen minutes late. She was convinced we had drunk ourselves out of our minds, and then drove off of a bridge straight into Andrew Springs River.

"Sure, they will after I'm gone. If I told them beforehand, I would have to deal with all of it, and I don't feel like going through that crap. I always said I was going to go off somewhere after graduation, and I meant the shit."

"But, Billy-"

His eyes lit up with excitement.

"Go with me, Mace!"

"What?" I said, almost starting to choke.

"Yeah, what do you want to hang around here for? What's there for you to do? You've said it yourself. It would be a blast. An adventure!"

"You're crazy! You're nuts! This would never work," I said, shaking my head.

"Why not?"

"This is our home," I said.

The truth was the thought of running off to New York City scared the hell out of me. I had barely been out of town. All I knew was Andrew Springs, and besides people just didn't do things like that. Did they? What about your family and friends?

But deep down there was a part of me that wanted to say, "Yes, Billy, there is nothing I would like more than to leave this town with you."

"There's nothing here for our kind," he said.

He looked away from me.

I felt my stomach flip when he said that. I wondered if he meant what I thought he might.

"What do you mean?" I asked.

I hoped and prayed he would open up.

"Look, do you want to come with me or not?" he demanded.

"This is a lot to decide," I said.

My mind spun. How could I ever make it on my own in such a huge place where I knew no one or nothing? How was Billy going to do it?

"Well, I'm going. You can decide for yourself what you want to do. I'm going!"

And with that he picked his bag back up and headed back into the wild flowers.

"Remember this is our secret, Mace. Our secret, okay?" he said, staring me down.

"I won't tell anyone," I promised.

I sat there for a little while longer watching him pick and choose more flowers for his extra credit biology project. I wondered if I could ever be as brave as Billy.

A crotchety old woman, with bright red hair, squinted and looked down at her clipboard.

"Mason Hamilton!" Crotchety Old Woman called out.

"That's me," I said.

I grabbed my sax case and stood up.

"You're up," she said dryly.

She opened the door to the auditorium and motioned for me to go inside

The judges had come to our high school for the auditions. Rumor had it there were maybe only two or three scholarships open. I prayed to God that I would be one of them. I was the next to last person to audition. The only other person left was Hastings McDaniels, a guy who always seemed more interested in reading his comic books and picking his nose in band class rather than practicing. I didn't think he'd be much competition.

"Good luck," Hastings said, smacking on bubble gum.

"Thanks," I said.

I followed Crotchety Old Woman into our high school gym.

I walked into the auditorium, and there were two judges sitting behind a small folding table. The area still had a smell of stale sweat from the PE class earlier that day, and both of the judges had weary looks on their face.

The first judge was an older man who wore a tweed jacket and a bad, dark brown toupee. He had one of those handlebar mustaches, that until that point, I had only seen in old movies.

The second one was a younger man, probably in his early thirties. What little gaydar I had at that time went off. He wore a very bright red shirt, which was just a little too tight. Every strand of his wavy, milk chocolate brown hair was in the perfect place, and he was chewing on the end of his pen. He sighed and took a look at his clipboard.

"Mason Hamilton?" he said, while looking me up and down, from head to toe.

"Yes," I answered.

"What are you going to play for us today?" he asked.

He smiled a little too friendly.

I began to feel a little uneasy under this man's stare.

"I'm going to play that Amy Grant song, *I Will Remember You*," I answered.

He sighed loudly again. I guessed that a few of my fellow competitors had also chosen this song.

I glanced at the other judge who was saying nothing. He looked like he was about to fall asleep at any moment, and his toupee was slightly crooked.

"Well, go ahead," Red Shirt Judge said.

I took my sax carefully out of its case. I had been practicing almost non-stop for days now to the point that my mother told me to go someplace else. She said she was sick of hearing the same song over and over. I had even taken the time to buy new reeds the day before, which was one of the things I tended to put off.

I brought the sax up to my lips, and I played the hell out of that song. Well, as much as I could play the hell out of a cheesy ballad factoring in that I was a high school student that just started practicing again.

As I finished, I cautiously looked at the judges to see if I could read any of their reaction. Unfortunately, their faces were just blank slates.

"Thank you, Mr. Hamilton. You will receive notification by mail in a few weeks," Red Shirt Judge said, obviously dismissing me.

I quickly put my sax back in its case and walked out. I thought about how much that one moment might end up defining my future. I based everything on an Amy Grant song.

"Mason, are you not ready yet?' my mother said.

She looked like she might hyperventilate.

"Mom, I have plenty of time. We're not even leaving for the church for another hour and half," I protested.

After bargaining with the local pastor and making a sizable donation, my mother managed to book our church for Cherie's wedding with just a couple of week's notice. She was determined that her daughter would be married in a house of God. She then rushed and managed to organize a reception in one of the church's meeting rooms. She took Cherie to a bridal shop in Jackson where they purchased a simple wedding dress. The whole time my father warned that too much money better not have been spent, or they could just go off and elope.

Apparently, Houston's parents were so angry they made my father look like he took it well. So they were no help.

"Please, Mason, don't argue with me," my mother said.

She pulled her orange curlers out of her hair turning it into a ball of tight curls.

"Yes, Mother," I said.

I headed down the hallway. I passed Cherie's room, and I saw the door was open. She sat on her bed staring out the window. Instead of looking like someone who was just hours from her wedding, she looked like she was waiting to be executed.

*"There was no call from the governor," the warden would say. "Your life is over."*

I walked into her room, something I rarely, if ever, did.

"Hey," I said.

I cautiously sat next to her on the bed.

She turned to me and looked just as frightened as the day I saw Dad screaming at her. My sister and I had always had sort of a strained relationship, since I felt like she got all of the praise and attention from our parents. Looking back on it, I think she probably thought some of the same things about me because I was the only son. But at that moment I actually felt some sort of stirring of loyalty towards my sister.

"Are you okay?" I asked.

I looked down and saw that her hands slightly trembled.

She looked up at me with not the eyes of a bride but the eyes of a scared little girl.

"I really do love him. I do," she said.

"I know. Are you scared?"

"Yeah, kinda," she answered. She seemed relived to actually say the words. "Hell, I didn't really plan on getting married right now. I always thought I would go on to win the Miss Mississippi pageant, and then of course Miss America, and then move on to land a successful modeling contract. Houston by that time would have turned pro, and he would have been named MVP of the year. Then we'd be engaged for a year, plan the perfect engagement party, the world's most romantic wedding, and then we'd get married."

"Wow, that's a lot of stuff."

She turned away and looked out of the window.

"It's the right thing to do. It really is, ya know. For the baby," she muttered more to herself than me.

"You're going to be fine. It'll work out."

She turned to me with eyes that began to fill with hope.

"You really think so?"

"Well, yeah," I said. I struggled to come up with some words that might sound good. "Remember that time you were trying to get your cheerleading squad to do that triple pyramid?"

"Yeah?"

"And remember how hard it was, and how they told you it couldn't be done. But you practiced and practiced. You were determined to make it work, and you did."

She rolled her eyes.

"Mason, as great as that was that was cheerleading! This is marriage!"

"Yeah, but what I'm saying is that no matter how hard something is, whether it is cheerleading or preparing for a pageant, you always throw yourself a hundred percent into things. You find a way to make it work. I know you will with this, too. I just know it."

A small smile appeared on her face.

"I do, don't I?" she said, with that same wild look that came into her eye when she was devising ways to rid herself of pageant competition.

"Of course, you do," I said. I placed my hand on her stomach. "You and this baby will be fine. I just know it."

"Thanks."

"And, hey, I get to be an uncle! How cool is that?"
She began to giggle.
"And are you going to baby sit and help me change shitty diapers?"
I wrinkled my nose and laughed.
"I don't know about that!" I exclaimed.

Later that day, while I stood at the front of the church with the rest of Houston's groomsmen, I watched my father, reluctantly, walk down the aisle with my sister on his arm. I knew this moment was not part of his plan for Cherie. But then people sometimes do things to remind us that we have very little control over what others do. It doesn't matter what their relation is to you. You have to forgive them and move on.

I would also learn soon enough that I would have to forgive myself for disappointing some of the people in my life with actions I would take.

# CHAPTER 4

Easter break rolled around, and part of my grandparent's estate was just being settled. My mother needed Aunt Savannah to sign some papers. She told me she was going to drive down to New Orleans for an overnight trip, and I begged her to let me go along.

"Please, Mama, please, please, please!" I pleaded.

Since I was a teenager I only called her Mama when I really wanted something, and she knew it.

"I'm not going to be there for long. I'm just going for a night. Then I'm turning right around and coming back," she said.

I knew she was trying to make the trip sound like just business and no fun at all.

"Please, please!" I pleaded some more.

"Oh, all right. But you have to be ready first thing Saturday morning. I want to be out of here by seven."

I nodded eagerly.

I was surprised that she wanted to drive to New Orleans. I would have thought she'd want Aunt Savannah to come to our place. I think all of the recent drama with Cherie actually had her wanting to leave town for a change. My father, at my mother's insistence, told Cherie that she and Houston could move in with us.

My father had gotten Houston a job at the peanut factory, and my mother had gotten Cherie a job through one of her friends as a clerk at the DMV. The plan was that the two of them were going to live with us until they had enough money to be on their own.

I could tell that all of these life changes had gotten to my mother. She had become very quiet in the past few weeks. Usually Mother would have been too busy telling us all what to do with ourselves, but now her mind seemed to be off in some distant place all of the time.

"Seven o'clock," she repeated.

She got up from the kitchen table and walked over to the coffeepot to pour herself another cup. "I want to make sure we get there early enough before all of the sinners are out of bed and wreaking havoc."

The next day when I got home I checked the mailbox. I saw that it had arrived. Inside the mailbox was a thin, white envelope from the community college. It was their decision on my band scholarship.

I took the letter inside. Since no one was home yet, I just sat in the living room for a few minutes with MTV on in the background. I hesitated to open it. Not getting the scholarship would mean I would have to get some sort of job right out of high school and then try and decide what I wanted to do with myself. If I did get the scholarship, it would mean that I was indeed stuck here going to school. Either way, Billy was going to leave for New York, and I couldn't seem to find the courage to run off with him.

Finally, I couldn't wait any longer. I tore into the envelope and braced myself to read what direction my future would take next.

∾

*Dear Mr. Hamilton:*

*We are pleased to inform you that you have been selected to receive a full scholarship to Anderson County Community College for the fall of 1992…*

I stopped reading there and set the letter back down. I was about to make some hard decisions.

Billy began hacking as he attempted to inhale the smoke from his cigarette. "That's so nasty. I can't believe you're doing that," I told him.

We sat in his room listening to his new Black Box CD, and Billy surprised me by pulling out a pack of cigarettes some quickie-mart in town had sold him. Since he had just turned eighteen, he thought he should buy a pack and smoke them only because he could now do it.

When his hacking calmed down, he told me, "You can't tell me you haven't wondered what it would be like to smoke."

I eyed the pack of cigarette's sitting on his dresser and contemplated giving it a shot. I sat on his bed, which was never made, with my legs propped up on the chair that was in front of his computer desk. The room, as usual, was littered with clothes and old issues of *Rolling Stone* thrown around. On the wall was a poster of Madonna during her *Blonde Ambition* tour.

Billy was sitting on the floor next to his CD player he saved up all freshman year to buy. He wore only his boxers and a very old Banana Republic T-shirt. I was kind of surprised when he answered the door wearing only his underwear. He had done that a few times since that night we never mentioned. It only served to confuse even more as I tried to figure out what it could mean. Maybe it was he only trying to get a reaction out of me.

"Wanna try one?" Billy said.

He waved the pack in front of me, and then he began to choke some more.

"No, thanks," I said, trying to wave the smoke out of my face.

"Wuss," he said.

He took another drag.

"What are you going to do if your mom smells the smoke when they get home?"

He held up a can of air freshener.

"Did you think you were dealing with an amateur?" he smirked.

"You're nuts!"

"And besides, it's not like they'll be coming home soon," he said, rolling his eyes.

Turns out Billy's parents had a "date" once a month now where they would return very late at night. Billy had overheard his mother telling his aunt that she and his father would go to a cheap motel and have wild sex the whole night. She said it kept the sexual energy going. We couldn't imagine why people his parent's age would even want to have sex.

"I'm bored sitting at home every freaking Friday night!" he exclaimed.

He must have been getting used to the inhaling because he began to hack less.

"We could go somewhere!" I suggested, getting excited.

"Like where?"

"I don't know. The arcade or maybe we could go get a video?"

"Fuck! You're just way too on the edge for me!" he sneered.

He stubbed out his cigarette and leaned back against the wall in deep thought.

"Any suggestion then, asshole?"

He closed his eyes and breathed deeply.

"There is nothing to do here," he said. "If we were like the other guys in high school with girlfriends we would just go out to MacArthur Field and screw around. That's what kids in the country do for entertainment, Mason, they screw around."

I looked at him in his underwear and wished that I could go and do that very thing with him. Of course, I fantasized about it every morning, night, and sometimes mid-day. I never developed a crush on any of the other guys in high school, not even the burly football jocks, the track team members with their athletic bodies, or the artistic theater types. If I had any sense then, I would have realized that I might have actually been able to score with one of the theater types. But, oh no, to me there was no comparison to my blonde, blue-eyed Billy.

"Wish I had someone I could screw around with," I found myself saying before I knew it.

He started laughing, which made me angry.

"What are you laughing about?" I demanded.

"Nothing, Mace," he said.

He got up and sprayed some of the air freshener.

"I got that scholarship," I announced.

He stopped spraying for a moment, as if he was chewing on this information in his brain, and then he started again.

"Are you going?"

"I think so," I said, trying to sound upbeat. I hoped he would decide to go there, also.

"Well, we all have to make our own decision, Mace. If that's what you want, I hope it works for you," he said, putting a hand on my shoulder. "We'll always be friends no matter if I live here or in New York."

"You mean you're still thinking about going there?" I asked, sounding a little too desperate.

"I wasn't kidding. I meant it," he replied. "I've been doing more research. I think I'll try and get a job waiting tables or something to start with, and then see what happens."

"Aren't you scared to do this?"

"I'm more scared to think of what will happen to me if I stay here," he said.

He began to pick some of his clothes off the floor, an act that in itself was shocking.

I found myself becoming more and more upset sitting, watching him clean his room, and thinking about Billy leaving me behind to go to New York. How could he do this? How could he just leave me here?

"I gotta go," I said. "I have to leave with my mom early in the morning."

"Oh, yeah. Going to the Big Easy, huh? Maybe if you're lucky you can sneak away and go to some of the bars on Bourbon Street. When I went with my parents two summers ago, I did that."

"They let you in?"

"The drinking age is eighteen, and with my baseball cap and dark glasses they just let me right through the front door. It was a wild place. Real wild," he said. He gave me a look that there was a lot more to the story. But just when I thought he was going to tell it, he said, "Well, have fun."

The next morning Mother was surprised to find me waiting for her when she walked into the kitchen. I had my overnight bag sitting next to me, and I had just finished my breakfast of grits and toast.

"Well, someone is anxious," she said, pouring herself a cup of coffee that I had made.

"You told me to be ready," I said.

"I certainly did."

I knew Mother was impressed. Usually, she would have to practically drag me out of bed this early on a Saturday morning.

She seemed genuinely happy that morning sipping on her coffee and taking a look at the morning paper delivered from Jackson. She seemed happy at the prospect of a road trip. She asked me if I had checked the air in the tires and the oil. I told her that I had already, and again she was pleased that I was so on top of everything this morning.

Mother checked to make sure she left my father directions on how to warm up the casserole left for him. Everything in the kitchen was a great mystery to my father. My mother often said she would rather keep him out of it completely, or he might just set the place on fire.

A few minutes later, we were off and on the highway headed to New Orleans and Aunt Savannah. Mother turned on the radio and began to happily hum along to the music. As we drove, we went through one small Mississippi town after another. Sometimes Mother would pipe up and tell me stories about how she had heard that so and so had moved to this town or that one, or how she once dated a boy that lived in this very town. She had never talked much about her life before my father. So it fascinated me to learn that so many boys had courted her before she married.

"What about Aunt Savannah? Did she date a lot in high school?" I asked.

She chewed on her bottom lip for a second and then sighed.

"Not really. She never dated many boys at school," she said.

"That's weird."

"Why do you say that?"

"Because she's so lively," I said. "I would've just thought that a lot of boys would have wanted to date her."

"She was beautiful," Mother said," It's where Cherie got her looks."

"I've seen pictures of you. You weren't so bad looking yourself," I said, smiling.

She reached over and playfully slapped my leg.

"Listen to you. You keep it up I'm going to start wondering what you want from me."

"Can't I just give my mother a compliment?" I said.

She looked over at me with a look that said she was still sizing up my sincerity.

"Hungry?" she asked, about half way through the trip.

She took an exit off the highway towards a small town diner.

Usually my mother would have just driven straight through on a trip. It was another sign that she was in an especially good mood.

We sat down, and a waitress promptly gave us menus and waters.

"Ya'll take your time looking over the menu. My name's Lucy. Just ask if you have any questions."

Mother thanked her, opened up the menu, and began studying it as if there would be a test on it later.

"Look at these prices. I could cook all of this for much cheaper, and I bet it would taste better," she said. She shook her head. "Oh, well, we are on a trip."

"Exactly."

Mother took out her compact and checked to make sure her hair bun was perfectly in place.

"I'm glad we could take this little trip together," she said, shutting her compact with a loud snap.

*I felt a talk coming on.*

"It gives us some time to talk," she said.

*I knew it.*

Thankfully, Lucy saved me by making her way back over and taking our orders. We both ordered the hamburger steak with baked potato and cokes. Whistling, Lucy walked off to the kitchen to drop off our order.

"What did you want to talk about?" I asked.

"Well, can't a mother just want to talk to her son and find out what's going on his world?"

"I suppose," I said.

I started to tear my paper napkin into tiny pieces.

"With all of the recent excitement with Cherie, the wedding, the two of them moving in soon…"

I nodded and wondered where this was headed.

"When they move in it will be a big adjustment for all of us."

"Yeah, I'm sure," I said, cocking an eyebrow.

The idea of Cherie, her husband, and baby moving in wasn't something I was looking forward to, especially because I knew there was going to be conflict with my father.

"Everything's so busy," she said, reaching over and touching my hand. "You're graduating soon."

*It was the graduation speech!*

"I'm proud of you, son," she said.

I was slightly taken aback by her praise.

"Uh, thanks," I said.

"I know you got a scholarship," she said a little sheepishly.

"How did you know that?" I asked.

I felt a little violated. I wanted to share that news on my own time because part of me was still holding out on my decision. I was only going to tell my parents if I decided to take it. If not, there was no real reason for them to know.

"Well, you know Mrs. Banks's son works at the college, and she said she had heard…"

I was the victim of small town gossip.

"When were you going to tell me and your father? It's wonderful news."

"I was going to tell you."

"This is huge," she cut in.

Her eyes filled up with excitement.

"It's not that big of a deal," I said.

I wondered when the waitress would bring the food. I needed something to get off of this subject and fast.

"It means you get to go to college! That is a big deal!" she exclaimed. She then lowered her voice. "I wish your father and I could help you more, but money is so tight. And I know it's not fair, but with the new baby…"

"Don't worry about it," I said, trying to brush it off.

I felt like Cherie's needs were coming first again.

"But I do. You're a good kid. That's why I'm so happy you got this scholarship."

"But, Mom…"

"You'll be the first one in our family to finish college. The first one, yes, indeed."

"I don't know what I want to do yet," I said, trying to protest the fact that the decision seemed to be getting made for me.

"You can figure that out when you're in school. A lot of people do."

She looked at me with a look that made me feel guilty of even thinking of not going. It was that look that said she was glad she had done a good job, and she was relieved. Her child had a plan.

"Yeah, I guess," I said, meekly stirring my water with the straw.

"Now if we could just find you a nice girl!" she said.

And then, thankfully, the food arrived.

After making it to New Orleans, we promptly proceeded to get lost, despite the instructions that my Aunt gave us before we left. We quickly found ourselves in a neighborhood that didn't seem desirable. What looked like low-rent housing was covered in graffiti. The buildings looked as if a good wind came along they would just topple right over. People were practically all over the streets and sidewalks, but none of them seemed to actually be doing anything.

It was ironic when I saw a sign that said we were on a street named Desire.

I had never seen my mother so frightened. She tried to navigate her way through a city where the streets seem to go in circles, randomly change one-way directions, and switch names seemingly all without a reason.

"Turn off that radio!" Mother barked. "It's distracting me!"

I reached over and switched off the "lite" station Mother had just turned on maybe five minutes earlier.

She began to bite the nails on her left hand.

"I knew Savannah should have just come to us. I don't know what I was thinking. Dear Jesus, lead us on our way," she said.

"Maybe we could stop and call her?" I suggested.

"Are you crazy? In this neighborhood?" she said, her eyes darting all around.

Finally, we found ourselves on a street called Canal. Tall buildings surrounded us, and it looked like a shopping and business district. On both sides of the street were stores that sold everything from discount electronics, clothes, shoes, liquor, and tourist items. We passed a few big department stores, one named Maison Blanche and the other one named D.H. Holmes.

Streetcars ran up and down the middle of the street. The sidewalks, and sometimes the middle of the street, were covered with seas of people. Some looked like they were in a hurry, and others seemed that they had no where to go. They sat on crates or drank out of bottles that were in brown paper bags.

There were so many streetlights that sometimes we didn't know which ones were for our lanes.

Someone in the car behind us started honking their horn when we didn't realize the green light was for us.

"Move it lady!" a burly man screamed out of his window.

Mother was on the verge of tears. We were both very country comes to town.

Finally, by an act of dumb luck, after making a few random turns, we found ourselves in the French Quarter, at least what it looked like in some postcards that Aunt Savannah had sent me.

"I think this is it!" I yelled out.

Mother came to a screeching halt on St. Anne Street.

"Oh, please, Jesus," my mother muttered.

"257 St. Anne," I said, reading off the directions.

Traffic was thick down the one way street, and Mother tried to read the street numbers on the tightly packed houses.

"It has to be close," she said.

A car behind us began to honk.

"Maybe we should just park," I offered.

"Yeah, maybe…"

We both looked down the street, and we did not see a space anywhere. The cars were parked so close together that there were mere inches between them.

"Look out!" I screamed.

Mother hit the brakes.

At first I thought it was a woman, and then I realized that it was a very tall man dressed in women's clothing. Mother had come just seconds from running him over. He just decided to cross the street without any regard for traffic.

"Bitch!" he screamed, slamming his hand on the hood.

I saw mother glance to make sure that her door was locked.

After standing there for a second, the man finally began to move on, still cursing out loud.

Slowly, we began making our way down the street. In the distance I could hear blaring dance music, it sounded like a Madonna's "Express Yourself".

And then as if it were a gift from heaven, we heard my Aunt Savannah's voice.

"Sissy, what the hell are you doing?" she yelled.

She stood on the sidewalk in her trademark heels and a short red dress.

A look of utter and complete relief swept over mother's face.

"Get out of that car!" Aunt Savannah commanded, as she made her way to the driver's door.

Just as she requested, mother jumped out of the car and let Aunt Savannah get behind the wheel.

Cars behind us began to honk loudly.

"Shut up!" Aunt Savannah screamed at them.

She slid into the driver's seat and slammed the door.

She turned to me, smiled sweetly, and said, "Hey, Little Bit."

I smiled and tried to absorb everything that was going on around me.

Aunt Savannah hit the gas and sped up another block not paying the pedestrians crossing the street any mind. They didn't seem to care about her either as they crossed the street dodging the car, some of them with beer in plastic cups.

The next thing I knew, she slammed on the brakes and began to back up.

"What are you doing?" I asked, perplexed, gripping the door handle.

"Baby, we gotta park. Your mama sure couldn't do it."

In disbelief, I saw where she was going to park. It was a space that seemed too small for my mother's Corolla between a large pick-up truck and a parked taxi.

With little effort, she quickly, and barely using her rearview mirrors, parked the car in that tiny space in three quick moves.

She then looked in the rearview mirror and began picking at her hair.

"Lord this humidity is just hell on the do," she said.

She turned to me.

"Well, we should probably go get your mama before she has a heart attack."

"Yeah," I muttered.

I then began to laugh.

"Welcome to New Orleans," Aunt Savannah said.

We walked back up the block and found mother sitting on someone's stoop. She fanned herself with the paper she had written the directions on. She had a look on her face that a soldier might have after making it through a major war battle.

"I was beginning to wonder when you two would show up. I was looking out the window for you," Aunt Savannah said, motioning for us to follow her.

Mother stood up and took a deep breath. Summoning all of her strength to just walk, she dusted off the back of her dress where she was sitting, and began to follow my aunt and me down the block.

"This town is crazy," she muttered. "How do you live in such a place?"

Aunt Savannah stopped walking for a second, contemplating the question.

"I guess because I'm just as crazy as the rest of them," she laughed.

She led us to a big, black, iron gate that lead into an ugly, dark alley.

"This is where you live?" mother said, wrinkling her nose.

"This is it," she said. She opened the gate with her key and let us in.

We followed her in, and I found the place very creepy. An awning blocked all sunlight and the brick walls were covered with mildew. I saw a small plaque on the wall that said that the house was originally built in 1812. I wondered from the way it looked if anyone had done any renovations since then.

We followed her, and she suddenly took a quick right. I turned around and looked at Mother who was as perplexed as I was about where we were being led. And then I saw it. My breath was completely taken away.

The alley had led to a huge, open courtyard. Large gardens with at least a hundred different flowers were throughout. A tall magnolia tree stood in the center with a fountain and next to it a small koi pond. The craziness of the city, which was actually mere feet away, now seemed to be very distant. A brick staircase across the way led upstairs to the house that had a series of glass French doors all the way across. A large balcony with many plants also over-looked the courtyard.

Both Mother and I stopped in amazement. It was beautiful. Neither one of us had ever seen anything like it before.

"Whoa!" I said.

"Savannah, I never knew your place was this pretty," mother said, forgetting the earlier trauma.

Aunt Savannah grabbed both of the small overnight bags we had out of our hands and walked up the stairs.

"Well, come on upstairs you two! Don't be shy!"

When we entered, I was struck by the decor. Almost all of the furniture was white, and the carpet was a light cream color that gave the whole room a light, airy flair. Art prints in vibrant green, yellow, and purple colors hung throughout the room. They depicted scenes from the Mardi Gras with revelers in costumes trying to catch beads from the floats. Vases of fresh flowers, that contained every color of the rainbow, were placed throughout the room. On one end of the living room, French Doors opened out onto a balcony that contained even more plants and a set of white wicker furniture.

"Cool place," I said, plopping down on the overstuffed sofa.

"Hope you like it, Little Bit, that's where you're spending the night," Aunt Savannah said.

I smiled, happy to be some place new, some place different, and some place so alive with energy.

Unsure of herself, Mother wearily sat down on a love seat next to the sofa and fidgeted.

"You two can freshen up. Then we're going to dinner, and afterwards both of you are coming to my club for a show," Savannah said with glee.

Mother's eyes lit up with fear.

"Oh, I don't…"

Savannah walked over and placed a hand on mother's shoulder.

"No arguments, Sissy! You're not coming all of this way without me giving you a wild night in N'Awlins!"

Mother didn't look convinced but downright petrified. Everything that happened to her so far was much more than she bargained for.

"Sounds good to me!" I announced.

Savannah cocked her head and smiled.

"Now how did I know that you'd be up for it!" she said.

"Miss Savannah, so wonderful to see you!" a slightly plump black woman in a tight yellow dress announced when we walked into a restaurant, Belinda's. Aunt Savannah said it had the best food in the whole parish.

It was a little dive that would have been unnoticeable from the street, unless someone pointed it out to you. Savannah said you had to stay away from the tourist trap restaurants that were in the center of the Quarter. She said where the locals bellied up to the table is where you wanted to go.

"Belinda, baby!" Savannah said, placing a small kiss on the woman's cheek. "This is my sister and nephew. I told them if they were going to eat anywhere in town they had to eat at Miss Belinda's!"

"Ya got that right, baby!" Belinda said, looking us up and down, but smiling very friendly as she did it. "You know I'll take care of 'em!"

She grabbed menus and snapped her fingers at a bus boy that immediately set a table in the back. The place was dark and illuminated only by candles. We were led to our table, and I noticed how heads turned and people smiled at Savannah when she walked by.

"Hello, Miss Savannah," and "Evening, Miss Savannah," people said as we passed.

Savannah gave each person a warm smile and a hello as if they were a long lost friend. The whole place seemed to know her.

When we were seated, Belinda handed us menus.

"Oh, we won't need these. Just whatever you think is best this evening," Savannah said.

She tossed her blonde hair back and delicately placed her napkin on her lap.

"Will do, will do," Belinda said, rushing off to the kitchen.

Mother still looked uptight with her hands clenched in her lap and her eyes darting around.

"Loosen up, Sissy," Savannah commanded.

"I'm fine," Mother said, her voice lacking any trace of sincerity.

I was busy noticing how people kept looking back at Aunt Savannah as if she were some queen who had arrived to hold court. I had already seen how popular my aunt was throughout the French Quarter. While on our walk to Belinda's, we saw ads with Aunt Savannah with bulging cleavage and a huge smile, telling people to come to her club "for the show of a lifetime." Almost every tourist got told that a trip to her club was a must. I was sure that was one of the reasons Aunt Savannah always went out of her way to get to know everyone in the Quarter was to keep them on her good side.

"Their word of mouth to tourists is the best advertisement I could ever get," Savannah said.

As Belinda served us courses of steaming hot seafood gumbo, fried catfish, hush puppies, coleslaw, and for dessert creamy, rich banana pudding, Savannah rattled off stories about what was happening at her club, and how it was getting harder to find good employees. She had problems finding new drag queens lately. She related a story about how she had to fire two after they got into a fight that put one of them in the hospital. The whole thing had been over a wig!

I noticed out of the corner of my eye mother had begun to laugh slightly and loosen up. Maybe it was the food, which was amazing, and Belinda's hospitality that helped her become more at ease. She actually appeared to be having fun.

Next up, Savannah took us for a walk down Bourbon Street towards her club. At first Mother seemed horrified at all of the strip clubs, bars with people stumbling out, porn stores, and gaudy souvenir stores selling everything from plastic beads to penis pasta. Then Mother began to look fascinated with the scene in a way as one does when it comes to looking at a car wreck.

I, for one, was totally in awe. I had never before seen a place where sexuality was so completely up front and in your face. Back home, in polite company, sex was never even mentioned or acknowledged. It was if it never existed, and people's children just fell out of the sky and onto their front porches. The majority of people were so terrified of sexuality that in my eighth grade health class the chapter in our textbook with the words penis and vagina were ripped out. Here on Bourbon Street it was as if sexual images were thrown in your face, and they made it impossible for you to ignore them.

We neared the theater, and I caught a glimpse of something that I had never seen in public and had only done, of course, once in my life. I saw two men kissing under the balcony near a bar. Even though I was beginning to accept the fact that, yes, I was gay; I was startled to see such a courageous act out in the open for the entire world to see. I still couldn't imagine doing something like that. I had no idea how I was going to handle the whole gay thing. Growing up in my small town, I certainly never had much contact with anyone who was gay, at least not openly gay.

Oh, sure, there was Bernie, the hairdresser, who owned the salon where my sister got her highlights. I'd hear people around town make jokes about him being "that way", but in true Southern fashion people didn't really seem to say anything to his face, just behind his back.

One time I remember my father chuckling after we left his salon from picking up Cherie. He said, "Why would one of his kind want to stay around here? Don't they all go to San Francisco?"

There were times I wondered why Bernie stuck around, too. I'd see him around town occasionally, buying his groceries or what not. He'd sash-shay down the street with his spiky too black hair and clothes of bright blues, purples, and greens. He seemed, at least on the surface, oblivious to the heads that would turn, look, and then snicker after he left. Part of me admired the fact that he didn't seem to care much what people said or thought about him.

All I really knew of him was what Cherie said about his elderly aunt living in town. Apparently, he looked after her. I wonder where he met men. It certainly couldn't be anywhere around our town. Part of me yearned to ask him, to talk to him, and find out exactly what his life was like. But I was much too frightened to ever look in his direction for fear that someone would ask me why I had an interest in him.

Besides Bernie, I had only heard a few whispers about people, so I really had no knowledge about the gay community or how they lived their lives. Besides my suspicions about Billy, it was as if I might as well be the only gay person in the whole world-someone who was floating around, looking for their lost tribe, but never gaining sight of where they were.

So as I watched those two men make out, right there in front of God and everybody, for the first time I felt some sort of hope that maybe there was a life out there for me…somewhere.

I caught Aunt Savannah looking at me and smiling. I knew she had caught me staring at the guys, and I quickly averted my eyes.

Aunt Savannah's theater was right off of Bourbon Street on Orleans Avenue. From the outside it looked like a small place. The door leading in was painted black and next to it was the box office. I noticed a flyer that announced the shows were every night but Sunday and Monday at eight o'clock, and that tickets were twenty dollars a person. A sign above the building that flashed red and blue lights that read, "Savannah's Revue."

Once you went inside there were a hundred and fifty seats, which she said sold out most weekend nights with tourists. The seats and tables were black and the rest of the interior a dark red. Aunt Savannah explained that between songs the performers would take turns waiting on tables and serving up alcohol. She said her best selling drink was a mix of rum, fruit punch, peach schnapps, and garnished with three cherries. It was called the "Pop My Cherry."

Mother blushed at hearing the name and shook her head.

The theater was just starting to come alive. Aunt Savannah took us to the small backstage area, which contained a few dressing rooms, a lounge with a huge Judy Garland poster, and a tiny bar. It was nearing six-thirty and the performers were beginning to arrive. They were all very effeminate, and some of them, confusing to me at the time, actually had real breasts. They carried with them large garment bags that contained their dresses. The performers were a mix of black and white, young and old, short and tall, skinny and fat. Aunt Savannah would stop some of them as they walked by. They had names like

Suzanne Sugarcane, Marigold Flowers, Patsy Decline, and Martha Washing-tounge.

As if we were the oddities, they eyed mother and me curiously. Some would raise their eyebrows or squint their eyes as they said, "How do you do?" or "Pleasure in meetin' ya." Then they scurried off getting ready for the show and their waitressing duties.

Mother looked, once again, completely overwhelmed. She smiled and nodded.

"What interesting people," she mumbled.

Her eyes continually scanned the room. I could tell from the look on her face, with her wrinkled nose and wide eyes, she might have just as well landed on Mars. This world was that alien to her.

Even though it was different to me, too, I was intrigued by every aspect of it. These men were completely challenging any ideas there may be about gender and sexuality, and they were making money at it. It seemed utterly fascinating to me!

"Joey, com' ere for a second, baby," Aunt Savannah called offstage.

I assumed she was speaking to one of the drag queens. Instead, I was surprised to see a guy walk in who couldn't have been much older than me. He was a little taller, a little more filled out, and obviously of mixed race heritage-black and white. He had perfect skin, the color of equal parts coffee and milk. The contrast between his skin tone and his light gray eyes was striking.

I didn't get to look at his eyes long though, because they darted down when he saw there were strangers in the room. He looked shy and awkward. He wiped his hands on his pair of worn army pants and avoided eye contact with the strangers in the room.

"Yes, Miss Savannah?" he said, looking up again, but only at Savannah.

"Joey, this is my sister and her boy, Mason," Aunt Savannah said beaming.

"Hello," he said softly.

Our eyes met, and his mouth turned up in a half-smile.

"This is Joey. He's my stage manager," Aunt Savannah said. She walked over and put her arm around him. "I don't know what I would do without him."

Joey smiled and seemed genuinely pleased at the compliment.

"Nice to meet you," I said.

"Nice to meet you," he said, his voice picking up a little bit.

"This place looks like a lot of fun," I said, smiling as I watched two drag queens fight over a black wig in the back.

"You are not putting this wig on that nappy head!" I heard one of them say.

"It can be a handful here with our girls. Right, Joey?" Aunt Savannah said. She shook her head and watched the heated dispute.

"Yes, Ma'am," he answered. "I better go make sure the lights are ready."

"That might be a good idea," Savannah said, shaking her head in agreement.

But before Joey could leave, another guy, huffing and puffing, rushed in. He was probably mid-twenties, slender, with shoulder length wavy brown hair and dark eyes.

"Sorry," he said meekly to Savannah.

She raised an eyebrow and sighed.

"Beau, Beau, Beau" Savannah said, nodding her head. She walked over and put her arm around him. "Honey, I already know that you couldn't be on time if your mama's life depended on it."

"That's not true," he replied sheepishly.

"This is my front office manager, Beau," she said.

"Nice meeting you two," Beau said to us, with his eyes on me the whole time.

He then grabbed Joey's arm and began to pull him away.

"Come on, Joey. We better get to work before Her Majesty breaks out with the whips!"

"You should be so lucky!" Savannah said, with a hand on her hip and sass in her voice.

As Beau and Joey left, Joey looked back and smiled at me.

I think Mother may have picked up on some of the flirting. She cleared her throat and then sighed loudly.

"Well..." Savannah started to say.

But then a dressing room door swung open, and a sight to behold walked out.

"There you are, Miss Althea!" Savannah said.

Miss Althea walked over decked out in a bright pink hoop skirt straight from "Gone with the Wind." She was black, and from what I could guess maybe somewhere in her forties. It was hard to tell with all of the make-up on her face. In her ears were two huge gold hoop earrings, and she wore a long, curly, blonde wig. She was definitely a sight to behold.

"Um, um, um..." she said, eyeing me up and down. "Is this him?"

"This is my nephew, Mason, and his mother, Martha," Savannah said.

Miss Althea walked up to me, practically ignoring Mother, and held out a white-gloved hand.

"Miss Althea," she said softly, while batting her long fake eyelashes.

"Hi," I said.

She then turned to mother.

"Honey, you sure have a handsome son," Miss Althea said.

Mother put her arm around me and held me close as if to protect me.

"Thank you," she said sternly.

"Miss Althea is one of my most popular performers," Savannah chimed in.

"Oh, stop," Miss Althea said. She playfully slapped Savannah's arm. "Even though dear Lord in Heaven knows that you speaks the truth."

She burst out laughing at her own joke.

"Well, I must finish preparing for my number tonight. I will be performing Miss Diana Ross' "Endless Love." I hope ya'll are staying for the show."

"Of course they are!" Savannah exclaimed.

"Fabulous!" Miss Althea said.

She then scurried off.

"Quite a group of people you work with here," Mother said dryly.

Savannah smiled, looked at me, reached over, and tousled my hair.

"I'm so glad the two of you are here!"

That night Savannah had reserved us front row seats. As soon as she walked on the stage the audience went wild with applause. It was such a treat to see my aunt in all of her glory. She wore a short, tight black dress that had fringe all around the edges. Her ample cleavage was, of course, busting out. She opened the show and introduced each performer. She told a couple of racy jokes, including one about a priest, a rabbi, and a three-dollar hooker.

I finally saw why she was such a great performer. She owned the stage when she was on it, and she commanded everyone's attention. I even caught mother, in spite of herself, laughing at some of the bawdy humor.

Miss Althea's performance turned out to be the finale. She came out wearing her bright, pink hoop skirt surrounded by six buff shirtless men all wearing short shorts. I'm not sure it was exactly what Diana Ross imagined when she first recorded "Endless Love," but the audience seemed to enjoy it.

She took us back to her place after the show, and the three of us sat on her balcony. She somehow managed to convince my mother to let me join them in having a glass of wine. It was a balmy night, the smell of alcohol, vomit, and piss occasionally drifted through the air of the French Quarter. We sat on her balcony amongst all of the plants and looked down in amusement at all of the happenings on the street. It was past one o'clock in the morning, and the streets were still alive with spirited people who lived Saturday night to the fullest. Aunt Savannah, too, seemed to only just now be winding down. She took off her heels and propped her feet up on an ottoman.

Mother leaned back in her chair and closed her eyes. She seemed more relaxed than I'd ever seen her. She sipped her glass of wine and appeared to be enjoying herself.

"Sissy, maybe next time you can bring Elvis," Savannah said.

Mother burst into laughter. She never drank, and I knew the wine was going straight to her head.

"Dear Lord, I could just see him around here!" mother exclaimed.

We all laughed.

"He would be quite a sight!" Savannah said.

Mother slugged back the rest of her wine, opened her eyes, and looked over at me.

"Son, did you tell your aunt the good news?" she asked.

"Huh? What?" I asked.

"Little Bit, have you been holding back on your auntie," Savannah said, jokingly shaking her finger at me.

"Good news?" I said.

Mother began to rock back and forth in the rocking chair.

"My son is going to be a college boy. He got himself a scholarship to the college," mother said.

She peered over at me with a look of love and pride I had never seen before. I gazed down at the floor when I thought about the fact that I was considering not going when I knew how happy it would make her.

"Well, well, well," Aunt Savannah said. "You don't say? My nephew, the college, boy, huh?"

At a loss for words, I shook my head and smiled.

"He sure is," mother said.

She leaned back in the rocking chair and closed her eyes.

"Well, I sure am proud of you," Savannah said.

"Thank you," I said softly.

She shot me with a look that pierced right through to my soul. Somehow I sensed that she knew I was not as happy about all of this as mother.

"Well, I'm glad you got to come and see me before you started college. Then you might be too busy to worry about your old Aunt Savannah."

"That's not true!" I said. "I am glad we got to visit you. I like it here. I like it a lot."

Aunt Savannah nodded knowingly and drunk her wine.

I looked back at mother, and once again noticed how happy she seemed that I was her son. How could I let her down? I would be the first person in my family ever to get a college degree. That was how it was going to have to be.

# CHAPTER 5

Mr. Drexel was one of those high school teachers that you hated the most. He wasn't a pushover. He wasn't strict. He was just boring. His voice was completely monotone. He would sit in front of the class and for fifty minutes lecture on Mississippi history. Billy and I had both signed up for the class thinking it would be an easy "A". After all, how much could there be to learn about Mississippi history? Well, according to Mr. Drexel, a whole hell of a lot! He enjoyed ever single second talking about it, from the founding of every county, to his favorite, discussing former Mississippi governors.

"Don't forget that next week you will have to name all of the Mississippi governors in chronological order," Mr. Drexel said, with the first hint of excitement in his voice that day.

It was so boring I thought I was going to have to stab my eye out with my Erasermate pen to stay awake. Billy and I would kill some of the time passing notes back and forth to each other. Some of them would contain references to how utterly bored we were, or what we might wanna do this weekend. We'd do anything to try and make the time go by faster.

On the other side of Billy sat Amanda Thigpen. She had waist length blonde hair and skin that mysteriously seemed to stay tan all year round. She had also worn full make-up every day since the seventh grade. On the other side of her sat her identical twin, Miranda.

Amanda was considered one of the prettiest girls in school. She and her sister had co-won the title of Most Beautiful our senior year. You could tell she was used to always getting what she wanted by the way she carried herself. Amanda and Miranda's parents seemed to dote on their every need and lived to serve them. Their parents worked lots of overtime as owners of the local Piggly Wiggly to give them things like the Mustang convertible they drove to school every day.

Amanda set her sights on Billy at one point. I figured she was acting like a blind dog barking up a really dead tree, but Amanda had no clue. In fact, Billy's aloofness made her even more determined than ever to get what she wanted.

She expertly made key people at school aware of her fondness of Billy. The planned result, of course, being that Billy would hear about it and promptly make his way over to worship and help serve her needs. Billy seemed pleased over all of the attention, but he didn't bite.

I can only imagine how the stress of this must have drove Amanda almost to the brink of forgetting to have the roots done on her highlights. But she kept at it to the point of flirting with him, big time, in public.

Okay, I admit that maybe I was feeling just a little bit jealous over the situation. This girl could let the whole world how she felt about Billy, and I, of course, couldn't say a word, not even to Billy it seemed. However, I did take pleasure in the fact that he never fell for her charms.

Then Amanda did the unthinkable. One day at lunch she walked over to our table in the cafeteria, batted her eyes, smiled sweetly, and said, "So, Billy, are you going to the Peanut Festival Dance?"

A girl of her standing would have always waited for a boy to approach her, but she reached a point where she was determined that she would let the whole school see that she could get what she wanted.

Between bites of his hamburger, he replied, "Nah, I think they're antiquated events and just plain out cheesy."

"Oh," she said, obviously taken off guard. "Well, whatever then."

Practically everyone in the entire cafeteria was watching, whispering in disbelief. Could someone have really passed up on a chance to ask Amanda Thigpen to the Peanut Festival Dance, *the* big event before graduation?

She was devastated. It was something any other boy in school would have considered an honor, and he threw it back in her face.

Ever since then she had made it a point to ignore him or throw nasty looks his way. She was embarrassed that she had put herself out there to that extent, and she simply didn't know how to handle it. Since Cherie had beat in her the Miss Junior Mississippi pageant the year before, I was not on her popular list either.

After Mr. Drexel's class one day, Billy and I were walking out of class and Amanda was right on our heels. She walked right between us practically knocking us out of her way.

"Excuse me!" she said.

It was rude even by Amanda standards.

"She's such a bitch," I said under my breath.

Billy just laughed.

"I think it's kinda sad," he said.

He put all of his books into his locker. Somehow he never seemed to have to bring any homework with him at the end of the day. I didn't know how he did it.

"Want to come over to my place? I've got the new Janet Jackson CD?" I offered. I had recently become even more obsessed with spending time with Billy. If he really was leaving town, even though I wasn't completely convinced, I wanted to be able to spend as much time with him as I could.

"Thanks, but I recently smuggled in a New York Times," he said with a devilish grin. "I need to do some research. I only got a couple of weeks."

"Yeah, okay," I said.

I shut my locker and tried not to sound too disappointed.

"Catch you later," Billy said, taking off down the hall.

I felt a tap on my shoulder, and I turned around to find Sylvia standing behind me.

"Hey, stranger," she said. "Why are you looking so down?"

"Huh?" I said.

I watched Billy walk out of the double doors at the end of the hall.

"You had this look on your face like you just lost your best friend."

I shrugged my shoulders.

"Dunno," I said. "Hey, want to come over and listen to my new Janet Jackson CD?"

I noticed how much Sylvia had changed in what seemed like an instant. She was holding her books up to her chest, which I noticed had grown a lot bigger lately, and her hips had gotten much more curvy. I also recognized that she was starting to wear a little bit of make-up, just some base, eyeliner, and lip-gloss. Her usually wavy hair had been straightened to the point that it was silky smooth.

She had also begun to dress differently. Lately she had been wearing "girlie" tops and skirts. Gone was the girl I had known that had always worn baggy t-shirts and jeans.

I wondered when it had happened. When were we grown up all of a sudden?

"I was going to go to the library to work on my economics paper," she said.

"Come on!"

"But what the hell? I need a break," she said, laughing.

Sitting on my bed we ate potato chips, drank strawberry soda, and listened to Janet in the background. Sylvia had her eyes closed and swayed her body to the music.

"I'm so sick of papers," I said, crunching on chips.

She opened her eyes and looked over at me.

"Well, we still have a few more years doing it so you might as well get over it," she said. "When were you going to tell me?"

"Tell you what?"

"Tell me what? You know what!"

"No, I don't."

"Yes, you do."

"No, I…" I said exasperated. "Just tell me what you're talking about."

"I'm kind of hurt you didn't tell me beforehand."

I grunted.

"What?"

Sylvia took a dramatic deep breath.

"My mom ran into your mom at the doctor's office, and she told her you got that band scholarship."

My stomach all of a sudden felt tied up in knots. Now my mom was going around town telling people I was going to college in the fall.

"She did?"

"Yeah, why didn't you tell me we'd be going to school together in the fall?"

"I…uh…" I fumbled for words. "I just hadn't had a chance yet."

Sylvia looked at me with a look that said she knew that there was more to the story.

"Yeah, right. What's really up?"

The last Janet song went off, and I was out of potato chips.

"I'm not sure if I really want to go," I said meekly.

"Are you nuts?" she said. She sat straight up and brushed the hair out of her face. "You're being offered a free ride, Mason!"

"But what if I don't want it?" I argued.

"And what the hell else are you going to do? I mean, geez, Mason, what kind of future do you want for yourself? You want to work at the peanut plant with your dad?"

"No," I said firmly.

"Then what?"

"Is it such a crime to not want to go straight to college? It's not like it means anything."

"What the hell are you talking about?"

"Look at Louie, Mrs. Grant's son. He went all the way to Tulane, graduated, and now he just sits in her house watching "Price is Right." On the weekends, he gives out the rented shoes at the bowling alley. Where's his great future from going to college?"

"The reason Louie is doing what he's doing is because he's a lazy slob," Sylvia pointed out.

Sylvia had a point. Louie was a lazy slob.

"Yeah, but…"

"Come on, Mason. I mean, wouldn't you be the first person in your family to go to college? That's a big thing. I've known you since we were little kids, and I know there are something you're not telling me. Why don't you want to go to college?'

"It'll just mean I'm stuck here for that much longer. I want to go someplace else. I want to see other things. Billy…"

I stopped myself remembering that I had told him that I would not mention to anyone what he was planning.

Sylvia rolled her eyes.

"If Billy ate a turd for breakfast every morning would you, too? I mean, damn, Mason."

"It's not like that," I protested.

"I should have known he had something to do with this," Sylvia said.

I noticed a hint of resentment in her voice.

"What do you mean by that?" I said slightly raising my voice.

"It's like you're obsessed over him. You follow him around like you some little lost puppy. It doesn't make any sense," she said, waving her hands in the air.

"You're crazy!" I said.

I felt my heart beginning to race. I thought I had done a good job of hiding my true feelings for Billy.

"Ever since his family moved here it's like you've been under some spell where he's concerned. And let me guess, instead of going to college you want to do whatever he's going to do?"

"That's not it!"

"What are you…in love with him?" she spat.

My heart was beating so fast it felt like it would just burst right through my chest.

Sylvia stopped for a moment when she sensed that she had gone past a line into territory that I'm not sure even she wanted to deal with.

She reached down on the floor and picked up her schoolbooks.

"You know what? Do whatever you want, but I think you'll be making a big mistake if you base your future on whatever Billy Harris is doing."

"That's not what I'm doing," I mumbled with my head down. I knew what I said sounded more than a little unconvincing.

"I'm going to the library," she said. She headed towards my bedroom door and then turned around. "I really hope you think about your future."

She walked out and shut the door.

I lied down and buried my face in my pillow and moaned.

The last few weeks before graduation flew by so fast. Before I knew it I was being fitted for my cap and gown. Also, the whole family was adjusting to having Cherie and Houston in the house. I had had the horrible experience of overhearing them have sex one night through my bedroom wall. It's a wonder I didn't need therapy after that one. *Disturbing.*

My dad became a man of even fewer words after they moved in with us. He spent most of his days looking sad and old for his years, and I swear most of his hair seemed to turn gray overnight.

My mother threw herself into decorating our breakfast room into what would turn into the baby's nursery. Gone was the breakfast table and thirteen-inch black and white we often watched the morning news on. Replacing it was a crib, changing table, and teddy bear wallpaper. She did what she could to feel excited about the change in events. Cherie and Houston tried to act excited, too. But I could see the uncertainty in their eyes as they just looked at the new nursery.

I finally made up my mind to accept the fact that I would take the band scholarship. It seemed as good of a plan as any at the time, and I knew it would make my mother happy.

"So you're taking it?" Billy asked me, while we sat in the swing in my parent's backyard.

"Yeah, I figure I might as well," I answered.

The sun set and night took over. Billy leaned back in the swing facing up towards the sky and looked at the bats that flew around towards the tops of the pine trees. For some reason he always got a kick watching them fly around as dusk settled. I just thought they were freaky.

The mosquitoes, which seemed to be made up of nothing but teeth and wings, were out in full force. Nevertheless, we didn't mind as we just swung back and forth in the swing. But I had sensed from the moment that he had popped by my house that something was different with him, something was wrong. He had a distant look in his eye. I could tell his mind was light years away.

"Yeah, you might as well," he said, surprising me.

I was hoping he would beg me to take off with him to New York, and "roll the dice, and take a gamble" as he would say. Instead he just nodded and didn't seem to care one way or the other.

"You think I'm doing the right thing?" I asked, hoping that he would say hell no.

He shrugged his shoulders.

"Hey, it's your life. Maybe it is the best thing for you. An education certainly can't hurt."

"And what about you? Are you still planning on running away?"

He turned around and looked at me his face flushing red with anger.

"I'm not running away!" he exclaimed.

"I didn't mean it that way!" I protested.

He shrugged his shoulders.

"Whatever," he said under his breath.

He then stretched his arms up above his head and let out a yawn, and when he did his shirt raised up. I looked down and saw that his stomach had blue and purple bruises on it.

"Christ! What happened to you?"

He quickly pulled his shirt back down.

"It's nothing," he said.

I could tell by the way that he wouldn't make eye contact with me that there was something to it. It was him who had always said that you couldn't trust anyone who wouldn't look you in your eye.

I reached over and tried to pull his shirt back up.

"What the fuck are you doing?" he yelled, trying to push away.

He looked at me, and I saw the genuine fear in his eyes.

"Billy, what happened to you?" I demanded.

"I told you it's nothing."

"Nothing doesn't give you bruises like that!"

We heard my parent's back door open. Through the screen we could see my mother standing there with a dishrag draped over her shoulders.

"You boys want any ice cream?" she yelled out.

I knew better. She had probably heard us arguing and was checking things out.

"Nah, thanks though," I said, answering for both of us.

Billy folded his arms across his chest and started rocking in the swing again.

Mother paused for a second then she said," Okay. If you decide you do, you know where it's at."

"Thanks!" I called back.

She then shut the door.

"I should probably be getting home," Billy said, starting to stand up.

I put a firm grip on his arm.

"Sit back down," I said.

Taken aback by my insistence, I had never been known to be the forceful type, he sat back down.

"I'm serious, Billy," I began, "I'm not going to let you leave until you tell me what happened to you."

His eyes began to well up with tears, but I could tell that he was fighting them back. I had never once seen him cry. In fact, I had never seen him come close. Even when his grandfather died, whom I knew he loved a lot, I never saw him shed a tear.

"I need you to do me a favor," he said.

"What is it?" I said.

I placed a hand on his leg.

He looked down at my hand, but he didn't move it.

"The night we graduate I need you to help me."

"Help you with what?

He took a deep breath and lost control for a second when a single tear began to run down his right cheek. He quickly wiped it away and cleared his throat.

"My old man came into my room the other night to tell me that I had forgotten to take out the garbage, and..."

He was having difficulty, and I had thought we could tell each other anything.

"And?"

"He saw my New York book on the bed, and he was like, he started laughing, and he asks me what the hell it is."

"Oh, shit."

Billy then laughed, not the kind of laugh you do when something is funny, but the kind of laugh you do when you're reminded that life can suck sometimes.

"So I was like, what the hell? So I told him. I told him I was leaving the day after graduation and moving to New York," Billy said, starting to wave his hands around. "He tells me the hell I am, and I don't know shit about what I'm talking about. He tells me he's working on getting me a job at my Uncle Bert's mechanics shop so that I can learn a trade. I told him I don't want to be a fucking mechanic, and that I was going to New York."

He rested his hands in his lap now, but when I looked down I could see that they were shaking.

"Well, then he starts screaming about how I'm going to do what he says because I don't have a clue. My mom runs in and she's trying to calm him down and stuff. I looked at him right in the face, and I told him he could go fuck off."

"Whoa," I said.

Billy's father was an ex-marine and built like a football player. His personality also made my dad look like he just walked straight out of a Hallmark card.

"The next thing I know he's just punching the shit out of me and telling me I was never going to disrespect him like that again."

As gruff as my father was, I could never imagine him punching anyone, much less his family.

"My mom was crying and screaming, and finally she pulled him off of me. It took like half an hour before I felt like I could breathe right again," he said quietly.

I could see his eyes welling up with tears again.

"Christ, Billy! I'm so sorry!"

He just shook his head and looked away.

"Had he...," I paused scared to ask. "Had he ever done that before?"

Billy didn't need to say anything his avoidance of my eyes said it all.

In the years we had known each other, I had never once suspected. It was one of those sobering moments when you realize that no matter how well you think you know someone they can still harbor secrets that you have no idea exist.

"I didn't know," I said, shaking my head.

"Yeah, well, I didn't want anyone to know. He didn't do it all the time, just when he got really angry about something I did," he said.

He almost sounded like he was weakly attempting to justify his father's actions.

"You said you needed me to do you a favor?"

His hand, still slightly trembling, moved over mine where it ended up resting. His touch felt like an electrical shock straight to my heart. With everything in me I wanted to tell him that everything would be okay, and that I would protect him. I would make sure that no one else ever hurt him like that again.

I began to lean in and put my arm around him, but he abruptly moved his hand and the rest of his body a few inches away from me.

"I have to leave now more than ever. You understand that, don't you?" he asked.

For the first time ever he seemed to be asking my approval on something.

"Are you positive that going to New York is the answer?"

"I need to go make a life on my own, away from here, away from him, away from…a lot of things."

"Okay," I replied quietly.

"The night we graduate, right after, I want you to immediately drive me to the bus station. There is a bus that leaves at 9:00. I should make it just in time. We can put my luggage in your trunk the night before," he said desperately.

Luckily, for him, my parents gave me my mom's car, an eighty-five Corolla, when she bought a new one. It was a reward for the scholarship. They sure knew how to add on the guilt.

"Are you serious?"

"It has to be right after. The minute we get our diplomas I need to go. If my parents even catch wind of what I'm planning…"

He shook his head and cleared his throat again.

"I don't want that to happen. I just want to get that piece of paper in my hands and get the hell out of here. I know I'm asking a lot of you, and putting you in the middle…"

I put my hand on his shoulder, and this time he didn't move.

"I'll do it, Billy. I'll help you get out of here if that's what you want to do. You're my best friend in the whole world, and I really…"

Now I felt myself tearing up.

"I don't want to see you go, but I want you to be happy. I love you, you know."

I couldn't believe I had actually said it.

"Yeah, I know," he said softly. "Thanks, Mace. I won't forget this."

He leaned over and hugged me. He hugged me so tight I almost felt like I couldn't breathe. To feel his body that close to me, like I did that night, was practically magical. I would have done anything he asked of me; I was so in love with him. I was even willing to help him leave if that's what it would take for him to be happy.

He then got up and tried to compose himself.

"I better go home, but I'll call you tomorrow," he said.

I nodded and watched him once again as he walked away. Billy was going to leave. I was going to help him, and at the time I thought I had completely lost any chance of telling him exactly how I felt about him.

But sitting in the swing by myself, watching Cherie and Houston argue through her bedroom window about who had lost the remote, I realized that I still could tell Billy how I felt before he left. I could open those floodgates of emotion and just see where they might lead us. He would know how much he meant to me, and I hoped that that would be enough for him to stay.

For something to happen.

"There he is! There's my baby!" Mother gushed when I walked into the living room wearing my cap and gown.

The next thing I knew a flash of light almost blinded me as my mother started to take pictures.

"Mom!" I pleaded.

"Oh, let me have my fun!" she said.

She walked over to me and straightened the cap on my head.

My dad, to my utter shock, actually had put a suit on. I knew that had to have been my mother's doing. He sat in his chair, the burgundy recliner that had the tears covered with an off red colored tape. He put down his newspaper and peered over his reading glasses.

"Yep, look at that!" he managed to say.

Cherie, who was beginning to show, put some effort into how she looked, also. The past couple of months she had seemed to be turning into another person completely-a nagging wife, who complained about pregnancy related complications and ate weird things like pickles with peppermints shoved into the middle. Tonight though, she had made herself up like she did in her high school days. She had turned her hair into a cascade of perfect, smooth curls, and her make-up was flawless. She was even actually able to find a maternity dress that complemented her. For the first time she seemed to have that pregnancy glow that I had heard of but had never seen on her before.

Houston sat on the couch next to my dad's chair reading a hunting magazine. He, too, had gotten dressed up in a nicely pressed shirt and tie of which I'm sure was Cherie's doing. Since he had started work his muscular body seemed to be losing its tone, and Cherie was constantly throwing it up in his face. I did think she was being hard on him. He worked a lot of overtime to save money for them to get their own place, and I guess his workout schedule became neglected. However, he still ate like he worked out five times a week.

"Are we going to go eat now?" he asked, looking up from his magazine.

Cherie leaned over and slapped him on the shoulder.

"I'm the pregnant one, and I don't worry about food as much as you do!" she nagged.

"Houston, why don't you go fix yourself a snack before we leave?" Mother suggested.

She had been trying to play peacemaker in our household lately.

Houston grunted and made his way to the kitchen.

I felt a little weird standing in the center of the room in my cap and gown. My mother had suggested I put on the full ensemble for some picture taking before we left. She kept telling me to pose this way and that as I begged her to stop with the camera. I protested, but part of me liked all of the attention. Even though I sort of dreaded school in the fall, it was a nice feeling to have my parents so proud of me.

"Cherie, get up there with your brother!" Mother commanded.

"Hurry, I gotta go pee," Cherie said, standing next to me.

"Wait let me load some more film!' Mother said.

While she dug in a drug store bag, Cherie and I both groaned.

"You look real pretty tonight," I whispered to her.

She looked at me surprised and with gratitude. I knew that she had been feeling bad about her body since she started gaining weight with the pregnancy. To someone, like Cherie, whether it was right or wrong, she placed much value on her looks. This was a huge deal. I knew it probably had to do with her attitude towards Houston. I eased up towards my sister. I saw all of the things she was dealing with. I knew that she was trying to do all that she could to make it work.

"Thanks, little brother," she said smiling.

I felt her arm tighten around me when I heard my mother say, "Smile."

To this day that is one of my favorite pictures.

Sitting on the stage at graduation during the commencement speaker, someone who used to be a state senator or something like that, I looked across the sea of caps and gowns and saw Sylvia. She waved at me and smiled. The seat next to me was empty. Due to the alphabetical seating, Billy was supposed to be sitting next to me, but he was no where in sight. I grew even more confused when at a distance I recognized his parents sitting in the auditorium. Finally, trying to sneak on stage, drawing attention to himself in true Billy fashion, he showed up. The speaker cleared his throat, clearly annoyed, and then continued with his speech.

Billy sat down, elbowed me, and smiled.

"Where the hell have you been?" I whispered.

"Hey, I had to take a piss," he replied.

The previous night he had come over to my house and we put his suitcase in my trunk. His bravery amazed me, and he didn't seem the least bit scared. He was going to start a whole new life and all he had to take with him was what was in an old, black tattered suitcase which included a few outfits, underwear, socks, toiletries, a few of his favorite books and pictures, and some CDs for his portable player.

"Is that all your taking?" I asked.

"It's all I can bring with me on the bus, and besides," he said, slamming down the trunk. "I don't want anything else from this place."

He said he had located a youth hostel in New York, and he was going to stay there to begin with before figuring what to do next. He was sure that his parents didn't have any idea. His father had even arranged for him to have an interview where he worked.

"That idiot has no clue. He's convinced I'm going to be there Monday morning," Billy said. "I guess he thinks if he can get me a job working with him he can keep a better eye on me. To hell with that shit, I'm done with him."

It took a little convincing to get my parents to let me drive my own car, alone, to graduation. I had lied and told them that I had already made plans with Billy and Sylvia right after the ceremony. My mother seemed disappointed. I think she wanted the whole family to go out to dinner afterwards, but I certainly couldn't tell her the truth.

I was so lost in my thoughts I didn't even realize that they had begun calling names and handing out diplomas.

"Nate Ashbrook," the principal announced over the mic. "Patty Beasley."

Billy leaned over and whispered, "This is it."

All of a sudden, I felt my stomach do a flip, and I felt nervous.

"Finally," I muttered to Billy.

As if he were a prisoner suddenly being let out of death row, he looked over at me with an expression of extreme relief that I had never seen before.

"Mason Hamilton," the principal announced.

I heard applause, and out in the audience I saw my family standing up and clapping. Even my dad seemed overcome in emotion as he clapped wildly. I saw my mother wipe her eyes, and I knew she was crying.

Billy jabbed me in the side.

"Well, go on," he said smiling.

I got up and walked over to the principal who handed me the diploma.

"Congratulations," he said to me. Then he called out the next name, "Billy Harris."

Immediately afterwards, all of the graduates met their families in the court-yard in front of the auditorium. Billy and I walked out together. He was going to try and dodge his parents all together, but his mother saw us as soon as we walked out.

"Billy!" she called out, waving her hand, which held a camera high in the air.

His father stood by her side looking at his watch.

I looked over at Billy and saw him try to smile for his mother's sake. He wasn't talking about it much, but I suspected that he was at least in some con-flict about leaving his mother behind this way.

"Meet me in fifteen minutes behind the auditorium," he said, and then he headed in their direction.

I nodded.

"Over here, Mason!" I heard Mother call out, as if I couldn't see her jump-ing up and down just thirty feet away.

I walked over to my family, and Mother immediately threw her arms around me.

"I'm so proud of my boy!" she shrieked.

"Thanks, Mom," I said blushing.

"Son," Dad said. He held out his hand to be shaken.

My father the overflowing fountain of affection.

"Thanks, Dad," I said.

"Good job, dude," Houston said, slapping me on the shoulder.

"Thanks, Houston," I said. I noticed that he did look very handsome that night. I could see why Cherie fell hard and quick for him. Then, disturbed, I realized I was checking out my sister's husband. So I said…"So do I get a hug or anything?" to Cherie.

"Yeah, yeah, of course," she said. With her round belly between us, she hugged me tightly.

"Oh, I thought I bought that extra roll of film," my mother said, digging in her purse.

"Mom!" I moaned.

"Give me just a second," Mother said. She pulled packs of gum, bottles of pills, a couple of wallets, her reading glasses, and a Bible out of her purse.

Cherie pulled me a little over to the side and whispered into my ear," So where are you really going tonight?"

"What?" I asked, wondering where this was leading.

"I was talking to your friend, Sylvia, before and she didn't seem to know that you were supposed to have plans with her tonight. In fact, she seemed really surprised," Cherie said, cocking an eyebrow.

"I don't…" I started to say in a feeble attempt to cover my lying ass tracks.

"Ah, come on, what are you and Billy doing really?"

Whenever my sister cocked an eyebrow you knew she wasn't going to stop until she got to the real scoop.

"Found it!" Mother announced and saved me.

"Come on, mother. We've taken enough!" I pleaded.

"I'm the mother and when I say it's enough, it's enough!" she said, right before another flash went off.

After a few minutes, after much protest from my mother, and after avoiding Cherie's suspicious stares, I said my good byes and took off to meet Billy behind the auditorium. On my way I saw Billy's parents talking to the parents of Amanda and Miranda Thigpen of all people. They obviously had no idea at the time that their son was about to run off to New York, and I was going to help him with his escape.

When I met Billy behind the auditorium, he had already taken off his cap and gown and was smoking a cigar of all things.

"A cigar?" I asked, slipping out of my own cap and gown.

"Thought it was appropriate since we're celebrating a birth or a rebirth this evening," he said.

"Right," I said, shaking my head.

Sometimes his analogies were too much for me. To me, it was like, hey, you're just running away from home.

"Are you ready?" he asked. He stubbed out his cigar on the wall of the audi-torium and then dropped it on the ground.

"Yeah."

"Come on, before someone sees us," he said. He grabbed my arm and led me to the parking lot behind the gym where I had parked my car away from where I knew everyone else would probably park.

"Are you sure about this?" I asked for the zillionth time.

Billy said nothing, but instead just laughed.

"Hurry!" he commanded, practically beginning to run.

When we made it to the car he tossed his cap and gown on the ground, while I put mine in the back seat.

"I think Cherie is on the fact that something else is going on," I announced once we were in the car, and I got behind the wheel.

A look of panic swept over Billy's face.

"Well, then, come on, let's go!" he exclaimed.

As we were pulling out of the parking lot, we drove past Amanda Thigpen in the alley between the gym and the athletic offices. She was making out with her new boyfriend, Duane, a personal trainer, who wore two earrings, and had recently moved to Jackson.

As we drove by, her head turned and our eyes met. She saw Billy in the front seat with me. She glared at us suspiciously.

I hit the gas!

The whole way to the bus station we drove in silence. I tried to work up the nerve to talk to Billy about you know, my feelings, but I couldn't find the guts to do it. He just sat in the passenger seat, staring out the window with a blank look that I couldn't read at all. When we arrived at the bus station, five miles outside of town, the parking lot was practically empty. There was only one lone bus that looked like it had seen much better days. Black exhaust smoke sput-tered out of the back as the engine rumbled. A few scattered people, mostly young, were boarding already.

"It's not too late. We can turn around and go back," I suggested feebly.

He turned and looked at the bus, ignoring my comment.

"Wow, this is it," he said.

I started to reach for the door handle, and he grabbed my other arm.

"Don't," he said.

"What? Why?"

"Look, Mason, thanks for doing this for me. It means a lot, but at this point I need to do it on my own. Just pop the trunk. I'll grab my stuff, and you can take off."

I felt my eyes begin to well up.

"Christ, don't do this," he said. He shook his head and purposely avoided my eyes.

"I can't help it," I said. I let my tears run freely. "It's just after everything we've been through…"

His hand reached over and rested on my knee. My mind immediately went back to that night where we kissed and held each other. With everything in me, I wanted to just reach over and grab him and kiss him as I had that night. One last time to taste his lips, feel the warmth of his arms around me; that was all that I wanted.

Just before I conjured up the courage to do it, he quickly leaned over and placed a single kiss on my cheek.

"Bye, Mason," he said, before quickly jumping out of the car.

I sat there in shock for a moment not knowing what to do. In the rearview mirror I watched him walk around back to the trunk, and I remembered his luggage. I reached under the seat and pulled the handle to open the trunk. He reached in, grabbed his luggage, and slammed down the trunk.

As he walked towards the bus, he turned around one last time, looked at me, and gave me that Billy Harris smile, the one that made me melt. Before I could respond in any way, he turned back around and headed straight for the bus.

I sat in my car and watched him get on board. I sat and watched the final passengers get on board. I watched the driver board the bus and shut the door, and I watched the bus rumble as it headed down the highway on that warm summer evening. I watched Billy Harris, the boy I had grown up with, admired, and shared my dreams and first kiss with, leave our hometown behind to start a new life.

# CHAPTER 6

❀

The next day the real fun began.

"I don't know where he is," I told an unconvinced crowd.

In our living room, besides my parents, there were Billy's parents, Cherie, and Houston.

Mr. Harris looked at me with stern eyes.

"Son, I know you know where he is. Now you better tell us," he said in a raised voice.

"Maybe he doesn't know where the boy went," my dad, in a surprising defense, spoke up and said.

Billy's mother was standing behind her husband fighting back tears.

"I just want to know if my baby is okay. He left us no note or anything," she said, crumpling up a tissue in her hand.

My mother reached over and put an arm around her consoling her as I guess only one mother can do to another.

"Now that Amanda Thigpen girl said she saw ya'll leaving together right after graduation," Mr. Harris said. He sat next to me and lowered his voice. I guess he decided to try the nice approach.

As told to me by Cherie, Mrs. Harris was upset because she didn't know where her son was, and Mr. Harris was just full of anger at figuring out that he had been duped. They were asking everyone at the ceremony if they had seen Billy, and that's when Amanda Thigpen sauntered back to the crowd. She announced, very loudly, that she had seen Billy and I speed out of the back parking lot, as if we didn't want to be seen.

I had promised, make that swore, to Billy I would not say a word about his whereabouts to anyone. He said he would contact them once he got to New York, and there was nothing that they could do about it.

I tried to give my best lost and confused look.

"We came back here. He said he had to get something from home. He said he'd meet me at my place an hour later, but he didn't." I said exactly what Billy told me to say.

I looked over at his mother and watched her continue to cry. I felt so bad for her. All she wanted to know was that her son was okay. With everything in me I wanted to tell her that Billy was fine, and he was on his way to New York.

Like a gift from God, at that moment the phone rang, and my mother answered it.

"It's for you," my mother said. She handed the phone to Billy's mother.

Mrs. Harris looked in shock when she took the phone. A few minutes later we would find out that it was Billy's grandmother. She had received a letter from Billy, which he mailed right before he left, saying he went to New York and would contact her once he got there. I was off the hook.

A couple of days later, Billy kept his word and called his grandmother. He told her he was doing fine, and yes, he knew what he was doing. He said he was staying at some boarding house he had found, and that he would call her later when he had a more permanent address and phone number. I heard that his father was furious and actually vowed not to speak with him anymore if he was going to act that senseless. I must admit that I was a little upset. I thought that I would have heard from him, but not a word. I wondered what he was doing in New York and about what adventures he was having while I sat on the sofa and watched talk shows.

My talk show studies were cut short when one of my father's coworkers at the peanut factory put me in touch with his father who owned the local ice cream parlor. Before I knew it I was wearing a pink paper hat with matching apron at Spence's 32 Flavors. I guess they had to one up Baskin Robbins.

For twenty hours a week I scooped up ice cream, made shakes and banana splits, and cleaned up the messes of three year olds who thought it was funny to smear their ice cream all over the front window. For the first couple of weeks I just scooped the ice cream and stared out the front window at life as it passed by-kids out for the summer and people buying their groceries at the Piggly Wiggly next door. My mind, as sad as it was, would constantly drift back to

Billy. I wondered what he did in the city that never slept. He probably did something more exciting than cleaning the shake machines.

One day, as I noticed to my horror that we were almost out of Rocky Road, a guy walked into the parlor. I would find out later that he was exactly one year and a day older. He was tall, well over six feet, and had bright bleached blonde hair, just like Madonna's in the "Open your Heart" video. He wore a hoop earring in his left ear, and trust me you didn't see much of that in my hometown. He also had on a tight white t-shirt and faded ragged jeans, which looked like they could fall apart any second as he wore them.

I stood there for a moment not knowing what to make of this guy. His way of dress just screamed, "I am from out of town."

He walked up to the counter, propped both of his elbows on the counter, and smiled at me.

"Is your banana fresh?" he asked.

"Excuse me?" I said startled.

"For the splits? The bananas? Are they fresh?"

I had never been asked this question before. So I just picked up a bunch of bananas and showed them to him.

"Here they are," I said.

He eyed them as if they were diamonds, and he was about to make a major purchase. He ran his hands through his spiky yellow hair and looked back at me.

"Are they organic?" he asked.

"Organic?" I asked, not knowing exactly what he was meaning.

He rolled his eyes.

"I guess they'll do," he said.

"You want a banana split?" I asked.

"Well, yeah. If I just wanted bananas I would just go next door to the Wiggly Pig or whatever and get them. And make sure and put on extra whipped cream!"

He leaned more over the counter, and his face was just a couple of feet from mine.

"I like lots of whipped cream," he said winking.

"Uh, okay," I said. I grabbed one of the bowls to make the banana split.

He let out a slight chuckle.

"So what's there to do around here?" he asked.

For some reason, I wasn't sure at the time; he made me slightly nervous.

"Uh, not much, really," I answered.

"Yeah, no shit," he said, more to himself, and rolled his eyes.

Out of the corner of my eye, I could see him look me up and down.

"What do you do around town?" he asked.

"Uh, just kinda hang out I guess," I answered. I tried to avoid eye contact. I wished my stupid manager would return from the bank soon.

"Yeah, hang out," he said.

"You're not from around here?"

He put a hand on his hip.

"Ya think? What gave it away?"

I couldn't help but laugh.

"Just kinda figured," I answered.

I gave him his banana split, he paid, and then he went and sat in a corner booth and consumed the whole thing in what must have been record time.

Just as he left, Sylvia walked into the store.

He turned around, winked, and said to me, "Thanks. That was just great. It really hit the spot."

"Uh, sure," I said.

Sylvia gave him the once over as she walked in, and he exited.

"Who was that?" she asked.

"I don't know. Some guy that wanted a banana split."

She looked out the window and watched him walk down the street.

"That hair," she muttered. "He's gotta be gay."

I was startled and dropped a spoon into the sink with a loud clang.

"Dunno," I said a little too tensely.

"Well, I mean look at him," she said, still staring out the window. The look on her face said he might as well have been from Mars.

She turned back around.

"Heard from Billy?" she asked.

*Another sore subject.*

"Nah," I said. I wished, for once, that some customers would come in and save me from all of these questions.

"Wow! I'm surprised," she said. She walked back over to the counter and peered at the ice cream in the freezers.

"Yeah, well," I said. I took off my paper hat and scratched my head. "He's gotta be having more fun than I am scooping ice cream here."

"It's just for the summer. It's not like you'll be doing it forever."

"Yeah, it's just…I wonder what he's doing in New York."

Sylvia chuckled.

"He's so damn crazy who the hell knows," she said, pausing before asking, "Did I tell you I'm still seeing that new guy?"

"Nah," I replied. I stared out the window while she rattled on about how she wasn't completely sure about this new boyfriend. At least she got to date. At this rate, I figured my next kiss might happen by the time I was forty.

Then I saw the guy that had come in and ordered the banana split. He walked past the window and winked at me. Winked again! I wondered what the hell that meant. If he was gay was he, oh, my God, flirting with me?

"Are you listening to a word I say, Mason?" Sylvia asked, snapping her fingers in front of my face.

"Yeah, sure," I stammered.

Her eyes narrowed.

"Bullshit," she said. "Well, if you're just going to stand there all day dreaming you can at least fix me a chocolate shake."

That night I sat on my bed rubbing my wrists, which were sore from scooping ice cream, and wondered how fast this summer could possibly go by.

Cherie knocked on my door.

"Yeah?" I called out.

She opened the door and stuck out the phone.

"Billy," she said.

I immediately jumped to attention and sat straight up in my bed.

Cherie rolled her eyes.

"Well, here," she said, handing the phone to me and promptly leaving, shutting the door behind her.

I took a deep breath.

"Hello."

"Hey, Mace! What's happening?"

"What's happening with you?" I asked sounding, but not meaning to, annoyed.

"Just doin' my thing."

Like that answered my question at all.

"Yeah? Is that all? I thought I would have heard from you by now."

"Sorry, I've been a little busy trying to get settled here. Everything's going pretty cool."

I heard traffic outside and figured it was a pay phone.

"Where are you staying?" I asked.

"Well, I was staying at that boarding house, but at this bar one night I met this guy who just happened to be looking for a roommate. Isn't that the coolest? I'm like sleeping in the bathtub, but whatever. And I got a job as a waiter at a coffeehouse."

"Hey, your mom came over here last night. She's really upset. Your dad..."

"Hey, Mace, listen my time's running out. I just wanted to say hi. I'll write you a letter and give you my address."

"But, Billy..."

"Gotta go, man. Talk to ya later."

Next I heard "click".

I sat there for a few moments holding the phone kind of in shock about how fast it all went. I had barely had time to speak a word. I didn't get to ask him about how life was there. What was it like away from our hometown?

What was it like away from me?

The next day at the ice cream parlor I shuffled around and thought about my conversation with Billy, but then the bleached blonde guy walked in again. He pushed his sunglasses up on his head, squinted, and looked at me.

"How are those bananas today?" he asked.

Of course, the manager left, and I had to tend to the store all by myself. It had been a slow day since it was raining on and off. Obviously, the weather wasn't keeping this guy at home.

"Okay, I suppose," I answered, not knowing what to do as he just stood there and stared at me.

"I'll have a vanilla shake," he said.

"Uh, okay," I said, looking around for a clean ice cream scoop.

I realized there were none because I was just about to start washing all of them when he walked in. It meant it would take me longer before I could get this guy his shake so he would leave. When he stared at me it was like he could look straight through me.

Little did I know at the time that this was referred to as gaydar. At the time it just scared the shit out of me.

"Are you in high school?" he asked, suddenly as I was quickly washing one of the scoops.

"Just graduated," I answered back.

He drummed his fingers on the counter, watching me.

"Oh, yeah. How old are you?"

I laughed a little uneasily.

"Why?"

"Just curious."

"Uh…"

"What? Can't tell me? Are you really an undercover spy working in this ice cream parlor in a small Mississippi town?"

"Almost eighteen," I replied. I scooped up the vanilla ice cream.

Mr. Spence had spent a large part of the morning helping me work on my scoop technique. He kept saying it could be much more efficient.

"Almost eighteen, huh?"

"Yep," I said. I put the ice cream in the blender. I couldn't make this shake fast enough.

"I'm here for the summer," he began.

I felt a story coming on. I nodded politely and reached in the fridge for the milk.

"I'm staying with my grandmother. My grandfather died, and somehow I got roped into helping her out with some things."

"That's cool."

"No, it's not. It's dull and boring."

"Sorry…" I said, starting up the blender. Thankfully, I knew that this would at least shut him up for a second. I wondered where all of this was going. I wondered when the hell Mr. Spence would return. I wondered what Billy was doing that very moment so far, far away.

When the blending stopped, sure enough, he started right back up again.

"At first I thought I would find nothing to do around this place, but then I met this guy…"

I poured the shake into a paper cup and put a lid on it.

"I met him in a rest…well; anyway he told me there was a place to hang out. Nothing too exciting. Not like Memphis, or shit, even Nashville, but some-place."

"One seventy-five," I said, pushing the milkshake across the counter.

He dug into his pocket for money the whole time keeping his eyes on me.

"Do you know the place I'm talking about?' he asked. His eyes narrowed.

"Uh, no. I don't know what you're talking about," I answered. I wished he would get his money together.

Finally, he pulled out two ones and slid them across the counter. I quickly gave him back a quarter.

"Thank you," I said.

"Well…" he said. He grabbed a napkin and pulled a pen out of his pocket. "If you decide you might want to go one night with me and check it out, here's my number at my grandmother's. Just try not to call after nine. There's hell to pay if someone wakes her up."

He slid the napkin across the counter, and I just looked down at it for a moment. The name Daniel was scribbled across the top and below it was a telephone number.

"Uh, okay," I said, not knowing what the hell else to say.

"I think you'd like it there a lot. Think about it," he said. He grabbed his shake. "Thanks."

With that he sauntered out and left me standing there looking down at the napkin with the scribbled telephone number. Part of me was scared to even pick it up. What would that represent? I couldn't even imagine calling. What did this weird guy want with me after all? It ran through my mind that maybe he was hitting on me. But me? I couldn't even think about anything like that. Besides I couldn't imagine so much as kissing any boy, besides Billy.

I saw Mr. Spence walk up the sidewalk, and I quickly grabbed the number and shoved it into my pocket before he walked in.

"Damn rain!" Mr. Spence cursed, walking in and shaking his wet, salt and pepper hair.

Daniel walked by again sucking on the straw in his milkshake. He turned and looked at me through the window as he walked by and smiled.

The next day I wondered the whole time if this Daniel guy would come into the ice cream parlor. The whole day I scooped out, much to Mr. Spence's delight, cone after cone of ice cream to small children and their weary parents. But the whole day there was no sign of the guy with the bright bleached hair.

I left work and went home depressed that it was yet another Friday night this summer that I didn't have anything at all to do. Now that Billy was gone and Sylvia always seemed to be with her new boyfriend, I was left all alone. I realized that I had never gotten close to anyone else in high school but the two of them. Now I felt left all alone, doomed to spending my whole summer scooping ice cream, listening to everyone in my house argue due to the cramped quarters, and waiting for college to begin.

When I got home, my dad and Houston were sitting in the living room eating huge bowls, of all damn things, ice cream and watching "Wheel of Fortune." They grunted a greeting to me as I walked by and into the kitchen where my mother and Cherie were cooking a supper of hamburger steaks and fried potatoes.

"Dinner will be ready in about twenty minutes," Mother said.

Cherie was cutting the potatoes.

"Feel free to help out if you want," she said.

"Not really hungry," I said. I threw my paper hat from the ice cream parlor on the table.

"Well, you have to eat," mother said, searing the meat.

"Yeah," I said.

As I went down the hall I heard Cherie say, "What's wrong with him?"

I went into my room and shut the door behind me. I then threw myself on the bed and wallowed in my depression. Was this going to be what the next two and half months were going to be like? Trudging off to work? Trudging back home? Watching Oprah in between?

A few minutes later my mother pounded on the door.

"Dinner!" she shouted.

I heard her walk down the hallway, and I reluctantly got up off the bed and emptied out my pockets on my nightstand; spare change, keys, and wallet. I looked down on the nightstand and saw the crumbled up napkin with Daniel's phone number. I had come close to throwing it away the day before, but something told me not to-not yet.

I sat down on the bed and smoothed out the napkin with the horrible handwriting and that phone number.

I eyed the telephone next to my bed and thought about it. The first time I reached for the phone I stopped myself and looked back down at the napkin. I was so scared to call, but then the thought of spending another Friday night bored out of my mind amongst my family was enough motivation for me to give it some serious thought. I had no idea what this guy was about, but what I did have was a feeling that he could certainly shake some stuff up for me.

Finally, I picked up the phone and began to dial, and on the second ring it was answered.

"Hellllllooooo," the voice said.

I recognized it as his.

"Uh, hi, uh, this..."

"Is this ice cream boy?" he asked.

I couldn't help but laugh.

"Yeah, it's me."

"I wasn't sure if you would call or not."

Part of me wanted to hang up right that very moment and to stay in my safe little world, but I was beginning to open the door so I might as well step through it.

"Yeah, well…" I said, having no clue as to what to say to this guy.

"So did you want to hang out?" he asked.

"Uh, okay. Sure. Yes."

"I have the perfect place in mind. It was the place I was mentioning yesterday. I have a strong feeling you'll like it."

"What kind of place is it?" I asked. I felt like I could vomit right there from nervousness.

"Just a little club right outside of town. Not too far."

"Club?"

He chuckled.

"It's BYOB anyway. Ain't that the shit?"

"Huh?" I asked.

"Never mind. Want me to come pick you up?"

I knew I would die if this flaming guy with the bright yellow hair showed up on my parent's doorstep. I could've just seen my father's expression.

"Uh, no! I'll meet you there."

"You'll never find it on your own. Damn place is so hidden-"

"Uh-"

"Look, you want me to meet you outside of where you work and then you can follow me?"

That sounded like a much better plan.

"Sure. When?"

"Nine thirty. I gotta get the hell out of here soon before my last nerve is worked."

"Oh, okay," I mumbled. "I'll meet you there."

"See you then."

"Hey! My name is Mason!"

But I realized that had already hung up before I had a chance to speak. This guy still didn't even so much as know my name.

The pounding on my bedroom door made me jump.

"What?" I called out.

"DINNER!" Cherie yelled.

I sat the phone back down and stood up. If I had only known what all of this would start.

# CHAPTER 7

When I drove up to the ice cream parlor, the sky began to drizzle. Despite this fact, Daniel was sitting on the hood of his Thunderbird smoking a cigarette. His hair was slicked straight back, and he was dressed in all black with a cross earring dangling from his ear. I parked and got out of my car hating the fact that the rain was ruining all the work that just an hour ago had gone into my hair.

Daniel looked down at his watch.

"On time," he said smiling.

He stubbed his cigarette out on the bottom of his black boot and jumped off the hood of the car.

"Hop in," he said.

I looked at the car, then at him, then back at the car, and then him again.

"Nah, I'd rather take mine, too," I said.

Annoyed, Daniel sighed.

"Look this place is out in the middle of nowhere. I drive like a whore escaping Easter Sunday service. Are you sure you want to try and follow me?" he said. He walked towards me with a swagger that implied that, oh, yeah, he thought he was hot. "Besides, I promise not to molest you."

He cocked an eyebrow and smiled.

I glanced back at my car and tried to decide what to do. After all, I didn't even know this guy. I had no idea where he was taking me. I had no idea what he might try and do with me.

Fuck it, I thought.

"Oh, okay," I said, walking towards his car.

"Smart boy," he said.

Daniel kept his word and drove like a maniac. We almost skidded a couple of times as it began to rain harder. Add the fact that it was dark outside, I had begun to wonder what the hell I had gotten myself into.

I clutched the door handle and tried to not look at the road.

"Am I scaring you?" he asked. He dug around in his CD case while driving.

"Nah," I said, through clenched teeth.

He took his hand out of his CD case and said, "Shit, pick something out."

I took the CD case and wondered where the hell we were going. We had driven out of town fifteen minutes ago.

"Can you tell me now where we're going?" I asked. I dug through the CDs that seemed to include everything from show tunes to heavy metal.

Daniel laughed.

"Ah, all right, ice cream boy."

"Mason. My name is Mason," I said.

He turned and looked at me for a second.

"Mason, huh?"

"Yeah."

"Like as in the canning jars?"

"Yeah."

He shrugged his shoulders.

I put a Bette Midler CD in the player.

*How can you go wrong with her?*

"So?" I said.

He continued to speed down the dark, deserted highway.

"Yeah, I was here about a week when, bored shitless, I went to the local library hoping maybe I could find some books on sex, drugs, or something that I liked. They didn't have anything there, but they did have a lot of religious stuff. Oh, yeah, anyway this older guy, like mid-thirties was sitting on one of the couches reading the newspaper. As soon as I walked in, I felt his eyes on me the entire time. It was so damn obvious."

He laughed and checked his hair in the rearview mirror.

"So anyway, just as I was about to leave I realized I had to piss. So, I go into the bathroom and I'm ya know taking a whiz or whatever, when the guy walks in. I was like, oh, shit! This guy is cruising me."

He turned and looked at me for a reaction, but I kept my facial expression blank even though inside I was shocked.

He continued.

"So I'm taking my piss and he comes and stands at the urinal next to me and takes out his dick, but he's not pissing. I glance down, and he's *stroking* himself."

On that one I did let out a little gasp of surprise which seemed to please him.

"So he wasn't really my type. He was too old, and he had a little bit of a belly on him, but it had been so long since I had seen another guy's dick. I was craving it! So next thing I know, he's motioning for me to go into one of the stalls, and I'm like what the hell, so I go in with him. He locks the door behind us, and he grabs my crotch. He tells me he wants to suck my dick."

"What?!" I exclaimed.

"Yeah, he wanted to suck my dick. So I told him no. Not in some bathroom library! So he tells me his truck is parked out back, and he can do it there. So I'm like, all right."

He stopped to take a breath for dramatics sake.

"So in the truck, after I come in his mouth, we're smoking cigarettes. Turns out the guy is married! Three kids!"

"Married?" I exclaimed.

*Shit, I was naive.*

"Yeah, married. Well, he starts telling me, not that I asked, about how he has the urge to just suck dick sometimes, and he can't like control it. Then he tells me that there is an actual bar where all of the local gay people go to, but you only find out about it through word of mouth. It's in the middle of nowhere. It's not really even a bar. You pay money to just go in and hang out, and you bring your own liquor."

I couldn't believe it. There was actually a gay bar nearby. I would have never even dreamed because I felt so isolated. I never imagined that there were enough of us, around here, to have anything.

"So I got him to write down exactly where to go and that night I went, and I found out he was telling the truth. The place is a total trip, a total dive, and I would never go there if it weren't for the fact that, well, there is no where else to go around here."

"And that's where we are going?" I asked. The shock now registered on my face.

"Yeah," he said turning to me. "You do like boys, don't you?"

I sat there in silence for a moment. I was in no way prepared for all that was happening, so fast, to me.

"Don't you?" he pressed.

"Yeah, I like boys," I said, almost feeling like a ton weight had just been lifted off of my chest simply by saying those words. I had actually just told someone that I liked men, a secret I had kept so deep inside me for so long.

"I knew it. My gaydar never lets me down," he said confidently.

We made an abrupt turn down an orange dirt road off of the highway.

"Gaydar?"

"Yeah, it's God's way of making sure we can pick each other out. Yours will develop."

That was just too much for me as I sat back in the seat and tried to take into account the fact that I was going to an actual, real, live gay bar.

But before I could think about it too much...

"We're here," Daniel announced, when we pulled up to a metal gate.

"This is it?" I asked.

"Give it a second," he said.

A few moments later a guy wearing a cowboy hat appeared at the gate with a flashlight. He peered into the car with his flashlight and smiled when he recognized Daniel.

"Hey, Scotty," Daniel said to the guy who couldn't have been much older than we were.

"Hey, girls," Scotty said. He looked in the car at me.

I smiled shyly.

"Hey, there," he said smiling.

"Hi," I said.

I guess he was cute in a country, ho-down kind of way.

Daniel handed him ten dollars, which he promptly stuck in his jeans pocket.

He then walked back to the gate and opened it for us to drive through, and I found us going down yet another orange dirt road.

"Where the hell is this place?" I asked.

"Almost there," Daniel said.

He came around another corner, and I finally saw it. It looked like a big barn and light could be seen through the windows. I could hear the faint sounds of disco music coming from inside. Looking around there was a good thirty other cars parked haphazardly all over the place.

"Welcome to Bubba Joe's," Daniel said snickering.

"This is it?" I asked dumbfounded.

"Whaddya expect?" he said. He parked the car between two hunting trucks.

I could see a few guys in jeans and flannel shirts, all of them about mid-thirties, standing outside the door smoking cigarettes with cans of beer in their hands. They all looked in our direction as we got of the car.

"You're going to be quite popular," Daniel whispered.

We began to walk towards the bar.

"Why is that?" I asked.

"Because you're fresh meat. Enjoy it while it lasts."

*Fresh meat!*

"Hey there" some of the guys said to us when we made it to the door. Sure enough, I could feel all of their eyes on me. Their stares could have practically burned holes in me.

Embarrassed, I looked down and responded with a meek, "Hi."

Daniel led the way in. We entered, and every set of eyes immediately turned to us. Everyone had a look on their face that seemed to be hoping that maybe we were their savior who had finally arrived. It was a mixed group when it came to age. I saw a couple of other guys maybe around Daniel's age. There were a few older men. Most of them seemed to be late twenties and thirties. I even saw a couple of awkward looking drag queens in ill-fitted dresses sitting at the bar smoking and sipping out of bottles in brown paper bags. In one corner was a jukebox which had Thelma Houston pleading "Don't Leave Me This Way", and in the other corner was a pool table that a few very masculine lesbians seemed to have congregated around.

There didn't really seem to be a bar per se. Instead, as Daniel said, everyone looked like they brought their own liquor. There was a guy behind a little counter serving soft drinks out of plastic two liter bottles and plastic cups of ice. When I looked down I realized the floor was made of just dirt.

*So this was gay life?*

I had never felt such intense stares from a group of people as we made our way across the room. Everyone's eyes seemed to follow us wherever we went. Some looked at us with suspicion. Some seemed to be looking at us with lust as they smiled or wink. Others just seemed to be curious as they sipped their canned beer. I got the feeling that new people didn't come around often.

We walked up to the counter, and the guy behind it reached over and gave Daniel a hug.

"Daniel, baby!" he said.

"Louie, how's it goin', guuuuurl?" Daniel asked.

"Guess can't complain," he said. "Who's the cute chicken?"

"This is my friend, Mason," Daniel replied.

"Ah, ain't he a young one. Fine and cute," he said. He smiled and revealed that he was missing a front tooth.

"Yeah, he's all right," Daniel said, elbowing me.

"Uh, hi," I said.

I felt myself probably turning every shade of red imaginable.

"You boys need some ice or mixers?" Louie asked.

"Nah, didn't have a chance to stop by the store," Daniel said. He leaned over the counter and smiled widely at Louie. "You don't have anything back there, do ya?"

Louie looked around at everyone who had finally at least decided to pretend to act like they weren't paying attention to us. Louie's eyes shifted back and forth as if he were deciding if he should reveal some secret treasure.

"I got some Dixie in a can you can have," he finally said.

"Oh, yeah? Would you mind just sparing a couple?" Daniel said. He leaned over the counter, obviously trying to work some sort of charm.

I guess it worked.

"For you two boys, of course," Louie answered.

He bent down and reappeared with two cans of Dixie beer.

"Thanks, Louie! You're the best!" Daniel said.

He popped open his beer top and handed the other one to me.

"Don't you boys leave without comin' and visitin' a little more," Louie said. He smiled his part toothless grin, and his eyes checked out my body from head to toe.

"Oh, don't worry! We won't!" Daniel said. He smiled and grabbed me by the elbow and led me across the room.

"Louie is the owner," he began to whisper to me as we were walking across the room. "I met him the first time I came here. He's good for a free beer every now and then but watch out. He loves to pinch young ass."

I flinched just thinking about Louie pinching my butt.

A couple of other guys, a few years older, made their way over and exchanged warm hugs with Daniel.

"This is Eric and Patrick," Daniel said introducing them.

Before I could extend my hand for them to shake it, I found both of them giving me hugs.

"Hey, baby, how you?" Eric said. He hugged me tight.

"We didn't know you had such a cute friend. Where you been hidin' 'im?"

"Shiiiiitttt, I can't give away all of my secrets," Daniel replied.

Yet again I felt myself blush.

The two of them immediately began to fill me in on their life histories. Turned out they lived outside of Tupelo where they both worked at a department store in the mall there.

"McRae's not JCPenney's," Eric felt the need to clarify.

They said they occasionally came out here when they grew tired of the bar there.

"By law the damn place has to close by midnight," Eric said, rolling his eyes. "And that's just when I'm ready to get rollin'."

Eric was super tall, over 6'4", at least, and very bulky. Patrick was short, not more than 5'6", and weighed no more than a hundred and thirty. The two of them certainly made a pair.

Daniel said he had met them the last time he was there. They drank beer and played pool when as Patrick said, "The lesbians weren't hogging the pool table like they always seem to wanna."

We hung out with them most of the night drinking our beers and listening to the juke box play what felt like endless disco tunes. I stood back with Eric and Patrick as we watched Daniel work Louie for more beers.

"He sure is a piece of work," Eric said laughing.

"How'd you two meet?" Patrick asked.

"He came into the ice cream store where I work," I replied.

"No shit?" Eric said. He swigged his beer.

Patrick looked around the bar and sighed.

"You're the first new person we've seen in here in weeks," Patrick said, giving me a smile…and a wink.

I smiled. I had to admit that the attention was nice.

Daniel walked back triumphantly carrying a beer in each hand.

"Am I good or what?" he said.

We talked, and I told them of my plans to go to the local college and how I had a friend that had run away to New York after high school. All three thought that was incredible.

"I couldn't even imagine that," Eric said.

The comment made me feel a little more like chicken shit for not leaving with Billy.

It amazed me to think that I was actually hanging out with these guys who all happened to be gay. To be so isolated for so long, now I was having a simple conversation with a group of guys, and we all just happened to be gay!

As it neared one o'clock Louie announced that the place would be closing soon.

"Ah, hell, I guess it means we got to go back to Tupelo," Patrick said.

"We better before your mama realizes her car is gone!" Eric said.

Patrick slapped Eric's arm, "She won't notice."

He turned to Daniel and me.

"Mine's in the shop, and what she doesn't know sure won't hurt her!"

"Ready to go Ice Cream Boy?" Daniel said to me.

I found myself very sad knowing that I had to leave my new friends then, and I would have to go back to my parent's house that was packed with people, but where I still felt lonely.

"I guess we don't have a choice," I answered.

We said goodbye to Patrick and Eric who were still arguing about who was going to drive back to Tupelo. On the drive back, Daniel said he would take me to Bubba Joe's again if I would like to go.

"Yeah, that'd be great!" I exclaimed.

Daniel chuckled.

"You're such chicken," he said.

"What does that mean? Chicken?" I asked.

Daniel cocked an eyebrow and smiled.

"Oh, don't worry. You'll learn soon enough."

We drove the rest of the way in silence. I was exhausted. I hadn't been up that late since Billy would sometimes stay overnight. We always spent the night playing Nintendo and eating Oreos.

When we got back to my house, Daniel said, "Call me later Ice Cream Boy, and we'll hang out again."

I walked inside and tried to be as quiet as possible. My mother was such a light sleeper. A mouse farting would wake her up, and the last thing I needed was Mother asking me about my night and where I went.

It was completely dark when I opened the door, and I was doing my best to slowly feel my way through the room. Suddenly, a light switched on. Startled, I jumped and turned around.

Cherie was standing there with a carton of mint chocolate chip ice cream in one hand and a big spoon in the other. She was wearing her Winnie the Pooh pajama top, which had an ice cream stain on the collar.

"You scared the shit out of me!" I said, regaining my composure.

"Where'd you go tonight?" she asked. She stuck a big spoon of ice cream in her mouth.

Her eating seemed to have tripled during this last month of pregnancy.

"Just out with a friend," I said.

"Who?" she asked.

"What the hell is this? Twenty Questions?" I asked. I sat on the sofa and took off my shoes. I realized that I smelled like smoke from all of the cigarette smoking at the bar.

She sat down on the love seat next to me.

"Just making conversation, grumpy ass," she said.

"Sorry. I'm tired."

"Who was that guy you were with? The one with the bleached hair?"

"What were you doing? Spying on me?"

I couldn't wait to get out of that house. I hoped that then I would get some privacy.

"I heard someone pull up so I looked out the window. *Damn.* You're sensitive. There must be a story there then."

I decided then that I should calm down a little so as not to raise suspicion.

"He's just this friend of mine I met. We were hanging out," I replied. "Besides, what are you doing up?"

I prayed she would follow the lead and change the topic.

"I woke up hungry," she answered.

"You're always hungry," I said, leaning back into the sofa.

"And you're always grouchy!"

I started laughing.

She scraped the bottom of the carton with her spoon and looked sad when she realized that she had already eaten the last bite.

"I'm still hungry," she muttered.

"Is Houston still snoring?"

"Like a lumberjack," she answered.

His snoring was so loud that it even woke me up sometimes, and I slept in a different room.

She got up and started to head back to the kitchen.

But just as I was about to get up from the couch, she turned back around and looked at me.

"You know, it doesn't really matter to me where you...uh..." she began.

"Do what?"

"Where you hang out and who it's with. I really don't care. It doesn't matter," she said, with a hint of sympathy.

I sat there for a moment and tried to figure out what the hell that meant.

*I was so clueless sometimes.*

# CHAPTER 8

❁

A few more weeks went by. I went more and more to Bubba Joe's with Daniel and hung out with Eric and Patrick. For the first time I actually felt a part of a group, and I was having a blast. A night never went by where I wasn't hit on a least a few times. I would always ignore it, scared to really do anything physical.

"You'll get over that soon enough," Daniel said to me. "Believe you me. Once you have a little meat therapy, that'll be all she wrote."

A few nights Daniel would disappear in the woods behind Bubba Joe's, only to reappear about twenty minutes later. I didn't even want to think about what he could possibly be doing. Yet each time he would reenter the bar, where I was usually hanging out with Patrick and Eric, he'd never reveal any details.

"I had to take care of some business," he'd say.

"Ummmm, I bet," and "All right now!" Eric and Patrick would usually say.

Each time I had to come home I felt myself become more and more depressed. Bubba Joe's was the only place where I felt like I could be myself. At Bubba Joe's I could check out cute guys without having to worry about being caught, or for that matter, beaten. I could even queen out on the small dance floor if I wanted. I could relax. Being home, where I had to hide the fact that I was gay became tougher and tougher.

Much to my delight, Aunt Savannah came for a visit right after Cherie's daughter, Lily, was born. We were gathered around Cherie's hospital bed, and Aunt Savannah came bursting in carrying a stuffed teddy bear so large it ended up taking up the whole back seat of my car on the ride home.

"Oh, my dear Lord," Aunt Savannah gushed. "She's beautiful, sweetie."

Cherie was lying in her bed cradling the baby with Houston sitting on the edge of the bed. I must admit it looked a little strange to see my sister acting all maternal. She was captivated by her baby. Houston, too, transformed into a doting father. Hell, even I must admit the baby was cute.

My mother always seemed to be rushing around doing whatever she thought was urgent at that moment. She had taken off the week to help Cherie. My dad, who was so upset about Cherie's becoming pregnant, was even won over by the little girl as he held her for the first time in his arms.

"I'm so tired," Cherie said to Savannah.

"Well, honey, of course! You just popped this little girl out!" Savannah laughed.

"That's a big bear, Savannah," my father commented from the corner chair he was sitting in.

She walked over to him and squeezed his cheeks.

"Just a big teddy bear like you, huh, Elvis?"

My father for once actually blushed.

She walked over to my mother and put her arm around her.

"Now, Sissy, anything you and Cherie need just let me know. That's why I'm here!"

"Well, there are some things we need from the drug store," Mother said, almost hesitantly.

She didn't want to give up one little thing that had to do for caring for her new granddaughter.

"Great! Just give me the list and I'll go to the drug store. I'll even take Little Bit with me," she said, reaching over and tousling my hair.

Driving to the drug store, with the top down in her convertible and Donna Summer blasting on the stereo, Aunt Savannah reached over and grabbed my knee.

"So what you been up to this summer, Little Bit?"

"Just working at the ice cream parlor," I said dryly.

"Oh, come on! No time for fun? I don't believe it!"

"Not much to do in Andrew Springs," I said. "Not like New Orleans. Who's doing your shows while you're gone?"

"Miss Althea. You remember her, right?"

"Yeah," I said chuckling. "It's funny that you refer to him as her."

"Sweetie, one thing you would quickly learn is to never refer to a drag queen as he when they are in full dress, and Miss Althea is always in full dress."

"I wish I could come spend more time with you there," I said dreamily, thinking about what chaos our house would be when the baby came home later that day.

"Well, why don't you? Do it before you start school this fall."

"Really? You mean it?"

"Well, of course. It'd be fun to have you around for a few days!"

I started to get all excited until I thought about my job at the ice cream parlor. I was going to stay there until the week before school started to save money. And it was true that I was having fun Daniel at Bubba Joe's, but from my last visit to New Orleans I got a small taste of what I knew would really be a whole new world for me.

"And I know how difficult it can be being different in a small town," she said.

*Different?*

"Different?"

"Well, yeah. I can tell you're special," she said winking.

I wondered what that could've meant.

*Again, I was so naive.*

"Could I go back with you when you leave tomorrow?"

For a second she seemed taken off guard, but then her face broke out into a huge grin.

"Of course you can!"

"What am I going to tell mother?" I pondered. "I can just hear her asking about the ice cream parlor?"

"How much longer would you have there anyway?"

"Just three weeks," I answered.

"Well, you can help me out at the theater while you're there, and I'll pay you whatever you would have gotten there."

I threw my arms around her, placed a big kiss on her cheek and cried out, "Thank you, Aunt Savannah!"

She giggled.

"Who's the best aunt in the world?" she asked.

"You are! You are!" I yelled.

"Damn right!" she said. She reached over and turned Donna Summers up.

"No way!" Daniel said.

He looked sad when I told him the news later that evening.

We sat on the trunk of his car looking out over Anderson Springs Lake and drank a cheap six pack of beer he had bought.

"I'm so freaking excited!" I exclaimed. I gulped my cheap beer in celebration.

"Yeah, I hope you have fun," Daniel said. He smashed his empty beer can on the trunk.

I realized that Daniel would probably miss me since we had spent at least a few nights every week hanging out for a little while.

"Hey, I'll be back," I said.

"But I'll be gone by then. Back to Memphis."

"Oh, yeah. That's right," I said, all of a sudden feeling a little sad myself.

I wasn't sure what I would've done that summer if Daniel hadn't come into the ice cream parlor and made suggestive comments to me.

"And who am I going to go to that hole in the wall with? At least I don't have to worry about you trying to steal my tricks."

Daniel was referring to my still intense fear of having anything to do with a guy beyond conversation.

"What about Eric and Patrick?" I asked.

"Like I said, at least I don't have to worry about you stealing my tricks. Those two are on the hunt, too."

"Maybe next summer we can hang out again," I said.

"Yeah, maybe, if I come back this way" he said.

He tried to act nonchalant about it, but I could tell he was down about it.

"Or I could come to Memphis sometime and you could take me to all of those clubs there?" I suggested.

Daniel always made the clubs in Memphis sound like paradise compared to Bubba Joe's.

"Yeah, that could be a plan," he said, conjuring up a smile. "I could show you some real clubs."

He then turned and looked at me right in the eye, and I felt like for a moment that he was actually going to lean in and kiss me. It had never crossed my mind that he could've had any sort of feelings for me beyond friendship. The guys he always went for at Bubba Joe's were always these guys that were a couple of years older and usually big and husky. Plus, I certainly wasn't experienced.

But just when I thought he was going to go for it, something I had a lot of mixed feelings about, he jumped off the trunk and dusted off the back of his jeans.

"We better go. I got to have dinner with my grandmother. It's meatloaf night. I can't wait," he said sarcastically.

He got back in the car and the whole way home we drove in silence as he constantly changed the radio station between pop, country, oldies and R&B. He'd hum along to one song and then abruptly change it.

When we got back to my house, he stopped the car in front of my driveway, and there was an awkward silence between us. He cleared his throat and turned down the radio. We both seemed to be hesitating, but then he gave me a quick hug.

"Thanks for making my summer a little more interesting, Ice Cream Boy," he said, attempting a smile.

"Thanks to you, too," I said.

I walked back inside and went to the kitchen where I found my mother and aunt. Savannah rolled her eyes at me and motioned to my mother who was stirring a pot on the stove. Somehow I already had a feeling about what was up.

Mother turned around and looked at me with a look that seemed about as far from approval as one could get.

"So you want to go running off to the Quarter for the rest of the summer?" she said, still stirring the pot.

"Why do you make it sound so bad, Sissy? Like I would let anything happen to him!" Savannah protested.

"I remember what that city is like! We were there not too long ago!" mother said.

She took the pot off of the stove and poured pasta into a colander.

"Mother!" I pleaded.

"And what about your job at the ice cream parlor? The one your father got you by asking Mr. Spence for a favor?" she said, hands on her hips.

"Sissy, it's not like he's scheduled to perform brain surgeries that he's trying to skip! It's ice cream for Christ's sake!" Savannah said.

"Please, do not use the Lord's name in vain!" Mother said.

Again, Savannah rolled her eyes.

"I just want to get away for a little bit before school starts," I pleaded some more.

"And I told you, I could use his help at the theater!" Savannah exclaimed.

"At that house of sin?" Mother said.

I was surprised because I thought mother had softened towards my aunt and her way of life after our visit.

Savannah turned red with anger.

"House of sin, huh?" she muttered.

"I'm going," I said, boldly standing next to Savannah.

"You're what?" Mother said.

I saw her eyes narrow which happened when she was especially pissed.

I could hear Lily crying and Cherie yelling at Houston to bring her a bottle in the background down the hall.

"I need to do this, mother. I want to go," I said.

"Well..." mother said exasperated.

"I'm sorry, but I have to," I said.

"Fine. Do what you want! But you're telling your father about the job," she said.

I could tell that she was very unhappy with me, but something inside me told me that I needed to do it.

I looked down at Savannah who was smiling at me. Luckily, mother had too many things on her mind right now than to worry too much about me going to the City of Sin, and for this I had Cherie to thank for getting knocked up.

# CHAPTER 9

The next day as we drove into the city limits of New Orleans, over the swamp-land, I sat back in the seat of Savannah's car and relaxed. We were here. I had finally gotten away from Andrew Springs-at least for a few weeks. My father was none too pleased about my quitting on Mr. Spence with virtually no notice, but like my mother he was too distracted and tired with what was going on with Houston and Cherie to argue too much with me. That morning, Savannah and I left not long after the break of dawn. She said she had to take care of some business as soon as she got back into town. So, I had spent most of the night packing and preparing for the trip.

"We're here, Little Bit," she said as we drove into the city.

I could now see the outline of the Superdome and the rest of the city's sky-line.

"Now I will be counting on you helping me out at the theater," she said, attempting to sound somewhat parental.

"Looking forward to it," I said.

She smiled.

"I have to stop by there first on the way home, okay?"

As we drove into the Quarter, I thought about how much fun I had the last time I was here, and I was anxious to do some more exploring.

*This time alone.*

We parked in front of the theater, and a young man dressed in a valet uni-form quickly walked out.

"Afternoon, Miss Savannah," he greeted her and nodded towards me.

"Hi, Ernie," she said. She handed him the keys. "We'll be about twenty min-utes."

"Yes, ma'am," he said.

We walked into the lobby, and the drag queen that I remembered named Martha Washingtongue (how could I have forgotten?) ran down the stairs that emptied into the lobby.

"Savannah, I needs to talk to you. I've had it with that bitch I'm sharing that dressing room," she said, both hands on her hips.

"I'll talk to you tonight. I need to see my bookkeeper."

"But Savannah!"

"Tonight. I promise!" Savannah insisted.

Defeated, Martha walked back up the stairs mumbling something about dressing room tables, scarves, and pumps.

"The talent can be a handful to say the least," Savannah sighed. "If you want to hang out here, I'll be back in a few minutes."

"Sure," I said.

Savannah walked up the same stairs the drag queen had come down, and I walked around the lobby. Pictures of performers, past and present, graced the walls. There were pictures of them on stage and what looked like those black and white publicity pictures the movie stars take of themselves. It was very quiet and sort of dark at this time of day. I began to feel tired since we had gotten up so early and drove for so long. So I sat in a red overstuffed sofa and laid my head on the back deciding I would just close my eyes for just a second. I think I may have dozed off for just a few minutes. When I woke up I found someone standing in front of me-looking right at me.

"Hi," he said awkwardly.

He quickly tried to look like he was there to do something else, and he began to straighten some programs that sat on a counter.

"Hi," I said a little startled.

It was the guy I remember my aunt introducing to me as Joey during our visit. He was just as cute as I remembered him, and he wore a mustard yellow shirt, that complimented his skin tone, and baggy green pants.

"Joey, right?" I said.

"Yep, that's me," he said.

He started work on straightening some of the brochures on other tourist destinations, but you could tell that he knew he had gotten caught staring.

"I'm Savannah's nephew, Mason," I said.

"Yeah, I remember," he said. He tried too hard to look busy.

"Nice seeing you again," I said.

He stopped for a moment and turned towards me, and I once again noticed how amazing his steel gray eyes looked.

"You, too," he said. He looked genuinely pleased. "Are you here for another visit?"

"For a couple of weeks," I answered.

He stopped shuffling the brochures for a moment.

"Cool," he said.

"Aunt Savannah says she's going to have me help out here a little," I said.

I stood up which made him go right back to work.

"That's cool. Let me know if you have any questions. I've been around here for a while."

He stood back and checked out his work on the brochure rack as if it had been an important job.

"Thanks," I said. I wondered why he seemed so nervous around me.

Savannah came down the stairs, and he looked very relieved.

"Hello, there, Joey," she said, smiling widely. "I see you're getting reacquainted with my nephew."

"Yes, ma'am," he said.

"Did you tell Joey that you'd be helping out here for a little bit?"

"Yeah," I said. "He said I could ask him if I had any questions."

"Thank you, Joey," she said. "Is everything okay for tonight? Did we get those lights repaired?"

"We're all set to go," he said. "Everything's been taken care of."

"I'm sure it has. Well, we'll see you tonight. Come on, Mason," Savannah said.

As I walked out, I turned back around and saw Joey looking at me again, and he quickly averted his eyes.

"Joey seems nice," I said.

We stood outside and waited for the car to be brought back around.

"I don't know what I would do without him. He keeps on top of everything for me."

"How long has he been working for you?"

"Just a little over a year, but he practically grew up in my theater. His mother used to manage the box office for me."

"Used to?"

"She died of cancer just a little over a year ago," Savannah answered.

I remember feeling so sorry for him. He seemed so nice. Sure, my mother and I had our disagreements, but I couldn't imagine what would happen to me if she were to…well, I won't go there.

"And he had no other family," Savannah continued. "So I've kind of taken him under my wing since then. He's always been a good boy."

She paused.

"I think you two might have a lot in common."

Before I had a chance to ask what that was, the car reappeared, and we hopped in. I was anxious to unpack and take a shower.

We started to drive off down the streets crowded with cars and people. We went past the gay bars I had seen during my last visit. I couldn't help but look inside as we drove.

"See you looking," Savannah giggled.

I quickly turned away, ashamed.

"Oh, it's okay," she quickly said. "I thought you may end up wanting to spend some time in that part of the Quarter."

I felt myself blush.

"Uh…" I started to say.

"It's completely okay, and I won't report anything back to Andrew Springs. Promise," she said. She reached over and patted my knee.

I took a deep breath.

"How did you know?" I finally said.

"Sweetie, I've known lots of different people over my years. It wasn't hard for me to figure out which side your bread was buttered. That was one of the reasons you wanted to spend some time here in the city, right?"

*Caught.*

I smiled weakly.

"Kinda," I answered.

"I figured as much. That's why I pressed your mother so much to let you come."

I had just come out to my aunt, and I had totally not been expecting to do so.

As we sat at a stop sign a horse and buggy went by. The driver was telling a young couple some story about the mysteries of the Quarter and how it had the ability to alter the lives of those that surrendered their soul to it-sometimes for better, sometimes for worse.

# CHAPTER 10

"Up, up, up!" I heard.

Savannah banged on the door of the guest bedroom.

"Okay!" I called out.

I stretched and yawned. I couldn't believe how well I had slept the night before. Today I was ready for my visit to really start.

I stumbled out of bed in my boxers and looked around on the floor for a T-shirt. I had taken clothes out of my luggage, but I had still not put them away. Once I found the T-shirt I slipped it on. I decided to forego going to the bathroom first to clean up, and instead headed to the kitchen since I was dying of thirst.

I opened the bedroom door and walked into the hallway, where various pictures of my aunt during the years were framed and hanging. Even though they looked as if they spanned over a couple of decades, she pretty much looked the same.

"Do you have any juice?" I called out.

When I walked into the kitchen instead of Savannah, I came face to face with Joey. He sat at the kitchen table drinking coffee and eating toast.

*Shit! I looked like crap! How could Savannah not warn me there was company?*

"Good morning," Joey said.

I could tell he was trying not to laugh. Obviously, I had a look of complete surprise on my face at the sight of him. I could only imagine what I must have looked like in my teddy bear boxers, T-shirt from a high school band competition, no socks on my flat feet, and my hair standing straight on end.

"Oh, hi," I said, obviously embarrassed.

When I tried to turn around and run back to the bathroom to make myself presentable, Savannah appeared and wrapped her arm around my shoulders preventing me from going anywhere. She was already dressed in a white pant suit, heels, and she smelled of gardenias. She was totally unaware about how humiliated I felt standing there looking like total crap.

*In front of a cute boy!*

"Morning, Little Bit!" she said. She placed a kiss on my cheek.

"I didn't know we had company," I said under my breath.

"Joey is being sweet enough to help me run some errands today, and I thought you could go with him so that he can show you around town."

Joey smiled weakly. He could tell I was dying standing there looking like I did.

"Oh, cool," I managed to say. "I should go get cleaned up."

Savannah looked me up and down.

"Well, I should hope so," she said. "Run along. Joey has to leave soon."

"I'll be right back," I told Joey.

"No prob," he said, sipping his coffee.

I ran back to the bedroom and pulled out of my luggage a new pair of jeans and a white polo shirt. I then went into the bathroom and was horrified at what I saw. Sure enough, my hair was standing straight up on end and I had huge purple bags under my eyes. I washed my face, brushed my teeth, and gelled down my hair.

Then I walked back into the kitchen still feeling a little embarrassed but at least looking better.

"Well, now that's better!' Savannah said.

"Thanks," I said, avoiding eye contact with Joey.

"I poured you some juice on the counter," Savannah said. She motioned to a glass of orange juice on the counter.

I gulped down the juice, but before I could get anything to eat...

"Well, you boys better take off," Savannah said. She turned to me. "I gave Joey some money for you boys to get a snack this morning and lunch later."

"Uh, okay."

I had no idea this was going to be an all day event.

Joey again looked a little nervous, but I had already figured out that he seemed quite shy, which surprised me because he was so cute. He wore a simple white T-shirt and a pair of faded jeans, but his body made the clothes look great.

"You boys have fun!" Savannah said, leading us out.

The next thing I knew she shut the door, and we walked down in her courtyard.

"Sorry about how I looked earlier," I said. "I wasn't expecting anyone to be there."

He laughed, but still avoided eye contact.

"It's okay. It's cool."

"Where do we have to go?' I asked.

We walked out onto the street, and for late summer it was a surprisingly cool day since it was overcast. It looked like it could rain at any second, but it was a welcome relief to the oppressive heat I had felt the day before when I had arrived.

"I have to drop off a couple of checks to some places and that's it," he said.

"That's all?" I asked. "Aunt Savannah made it sound like an all day thing."

"Well," he said. He chuckled a little nervously. "Your aunt asked if I would just spend some time showing you around today."

I felt embarrassed that this poor guy got roped into entertaining me for the day. My aunt was his boss so I knew he couldn't say no. I was determined to talk to Savannah later that day when I returned. What was she up to with all of this?

Joey led me to a couple of art galleries on Royal where Savannah had ordered some new artwork for the theater, and he had to drop off the checks for payment. They told us the paintings would be delivered later that day to the theater.

While Joey waited for a receipt, I browsed around in one of the art galleries. I had never been to a gallery or even a real museum. I didn't think the small museum that was dedicated to the Andrews family back home at the library counted. I was fascinated by some of the paintings. The detail was amazing from the colors to all of the little nuances that each artist had added. I was also fascinated by the prices! Some of the paintings and sculptures ran in the thousands. I wondered who had that kind of money just to spend on a painting. Then I wondered how much Savannah had paid because I figured that nothing there was cheap.

"Ready to go?" Joey asked. He folded the receipt and put it in his backpack.

"Where to now?"

"I'll give you the grand tour," he said smiling.

First, we went to Jackson Square where I remembered seeing that huge, old church, the St. Louis Cathedral, during my last visit. Today the areas outside of the square, which included a small park in the middle of the area in front of the church, were alive with activity. Mimes, clowns trying to sell balloon animals, artists painting quick portraits of tourists, and tarot card readers were everywhere. The tarot card readers who seemed to set up shop with just a TV tray and a couple of crates were the funniest, I thought. Joey told me if I wanted my cards read he could to take me to a "real" reader who worked out of one of the voodoo shops in the Quarter.

We then went to a bakery called Le Madeline where Joey bought us the best pastry I had ever eaten. It was topped with creamy icing and stuffed with fresh blueberries, and we ate them sitting on benches in the Square.

"Any place in particular you would like to go?" Joey asked.

I was watching the parade of people go by. The whole place seemed alive with energy, and I found myself so happy that I had gotten out of Andrew Springs. Back home the most excitement you could hope for is that a new movie would open at the show. But in New Orleans, and in the French Quarter, the energy of the place felt like that there would be boundless things for me to do during my trip.

"I don't think I even know where to begin," I said.

"I know where we can start," Joey said.

He grabbed my hand and pulled me up. I was a little taken aback by this physical gesture, but I just smiled and followed him down Decatur Street.

Along the way, he really began to open up as he began to feel comfortable around me. He told me he was born and raised in New Orleans. Of course, I already knew that because of what my aunt had told me, but I didn't tell him that. He said he enjoyed painting, and one day he hoped to save up enough money to go to art school. Turns out he had been to the galleries we had been to earlier that morning quite a few times, and he also liked going to the local museums. He said he was fascinated by everything an artist could convey with simple paint and a canvas.

We found ourselves along the Mississippi River, on what he called the Moonwalk. It was there we strolled along as the ships and tourist steamboats went by. He told me the current in the river was so strong that if you fell in the muddy, brown water you might as well "kiss your ass goodbye."

Tourists walked along with us. Some paused briefly to take pictures of the boats. A Japanese couple stopped us and asked Joey if he would take their picture. He did, and the young couple seemed so much in love standing next to a lamppost with the river in the background. I wondered if I would ever have that look of love and contentment in my eyes they had when they looked at each other.

Once we continued on, we went to where Joey told me the Aquarium was located. He said I had to go before I left because they had some really cool albino alligators that just had to be seen. We then went to the Riverwalk mall where there were tons of stores, from the regular mall ones to local ones selling things I had never seen before…

*Chicken feet keychains? Baby alligator heads? Yuck!*

I noticed how Joey would look into the windows of some of the stores with eyes of wonderment himself. I sensed he had never had much in his life, and he probably had never actually shopped at the Riverwalk. Yet, he seemed to know every single shop there and what they sold.

After we left the mall, we walked a few blocks down Canal Street along stores that sold a lot of what Joey called "tourist crap." Cheap plastic Mardi Gras beads, Mardi Gras masks, those weird little snow globes (snow in New Orleans?) and the like.

Joey, who had seemed so shy, had almost become a motor mouth. It seemed he had a story for every building and every street corner. My fears that he had been dragged into this experience by my aunt waned when he really seemed to enjoy himself showing me around town.

When we turned off Canal, and onto a street called Burgundy, he told me he lived in a small apartment just a few blocks up. He said the only way he could afford it was that my aunt paid part of the rent each month. He actually seemed to be getting a little teary eyed when he said that.

"My mom died a little over a year ago," he said.

"I'm sorry," I said. I made sure to act a little surprised. I wouldn't want him to think that Savannah had told me all of his business.

"She started working for your aunt right after she bought the theater. I guess I was born a little over a year after that," he said. We continued walking along what was mainly a residential area of the Quarter. "Ever since my mom died, I guess, Miss Savannah has kinda been keeping an eye out for me. I don't know what I would do without her."

"What about your dad?" I asked. I could have slapped myself later for doing so.

"Well…I never knew him," Joey said, his voice trailed off.

"Oh," was all I could think to say.

"Want to get some lunch?" he said, obviously trying to change the subject.

"Sounds good to me," I said.

He led me to a little deli on the corner of St. Anne and Dauphine. A rainbow flag, just like the one I saw above the two bars I drove by with my aunt, hung off a balcony above the deli. There was another bar across the street that had a rainbow flag hanging off of its balcony. When we walked in, I found the place full of mostly men. Was Joey taking me to a gay place for lunch, I wondered, and what was he doing wanting to go there?

*You practically had to hit me upside the head at the time!*

Joey picked a table for two in the corner, and we sat down. A few moments later a guy smacking gum, with hair a bright shade of red that I know nature doesn't produce, showed up. He pulled his order pad out of the back of his pants.

"Hey, girls. Whattcha want?" he said, between smacks.

"Can we get a couple of minutes?' Joey asked, just now getting the chance to open the menu.

"Okay, but Mama ain't got all day, baby," he said. He then headed off for the kitchen sash-shaying the whole way.

"Is this place okay for lunch?" he asked.

It must've been obvious that I didn't know how to react since I was staring at everyone in the place.

"Oh, yeah. It's cool. Uh...is this..."

"A mostly gay place?" he asked.

"Um, yeah."

"Yeah, I come here a lot with my friend, Beau, who works for your aunt, too."

I remembered Beau from the first time I met Joey.

"So I know the food is good. Is it okay with you?"

"Oh, it's no problem at all. Really!" I said. I tried to sound all hip with it.

"Sure?"

"Oh, yeah," I said. I glanced down at the menu, but I couldn't help myself from asking the next question. "So...uh...are you?"

"Gay?"

"Yeah?"

"Well, yeah. I am. I thought you knew," he said, looking awkward.

"Oh, it's cool," I said. I paused before I added, "I am, too."

A big smile appeared on his face, a smile that I had to admit maybe even rivaled Billy's. It was even more amazing because up until this point, I had not noticed it before.

"I kinda thought so," he said sheepishly.

I wondered if Aunt Savannah had said something to him beforehand, but before I could ask him. Gum Smacker reappeared and said, "Now are you girls ready?"

We both quickly looked at our menus and ordered. It was nice because I felt like maybe now I would have a friend that I could hang out with like I did Daniel back home. I spent the lunch opening up to him and telling him about my summer so far, meeting Daniel, going to Bubba Joe's, and how I felt that just now, in so many ways, I was just beginning to start my life. Joey found the stories about Bubba Joe's very funny. He couldn't believe that such a place existed in backwoods Mississippi.

"So," he said. He cleared his throat while picking at his turkey sandwich. "Have you ever been in love before?"

"Love?"

*Does obsessing over your best friend since the seventh grade count?*

"I don't know," I said.

"Guess you haven't had much time yet though, huh?"

"Not really," I answered. I decided to change the subject. "So do you hang out at the bars here, too?"

He shrugged his shoulders.

"Sometimes. I'll go through phases where I will a lot, and then I won't for a while. It can be fun sometimes."

"Coming from where I come from it looks like paradise," I commented.

"Quantity doesn't always equal quality," he said. He picked up the bill and walked up to the register to pay.

I felt like there was a story behind his last comment.

"Maybe we can go out together one night. I turned eighteen so I'm legal!" I said.

I got all excited when I remembered the drinking age was eighteen there.

"Eighteen! Watch out!' Joey said.

He winked and smiled at me, and then he said we should start heading back. He would have to get ready for work soon, and Savannah would want to give me my assignment soon.

I made it back to Savannah's and found her sitting at the desk in her living room talking on the phone.

"Yes, Sissy," I heard her say.

My mother already called!

When Savannah saw me she gave me a "you know who this is" look.

"Hold on. Here he is," she said handing me the phone.

"Hi, Mother," I said when I took the phone.

"Are you okay?" Mother said. Her voice had the same urgency as if I had been sent off to war.

I sighed.

"I'm fine, Mother. I'm having fun."

"Now don't give your aunt any trouble while you're there," she said. She acted like I was a three-year old she dropped off with a new baby-sitter.

"How's the new baby?" I asked, hoping to get her to move on to something else.

I could hear the pride in her voice.

"She's so cute, Mason! Just adorable. Cherie's tired though."

"What Aunt Savannah? We're leaving now?"

Across the room, Savannah looked up from the romance novel she was reading, one of those with the guy with the long hair and the woman with the heaving breasts on the cover, and looked at me like I was crazy. But then she figured out what I was doing and had to sustain a laugh.

"What's going on?" mother asked.

"Aunt Savannah needs me to go with her to the theater for something. I have to go. I'll call you in a few days. Love you," I said hurriedly.

"Be safe…"

"Bye, Mother."

I hung up the phone and took a deep breath.

"I can't believe she called me after I've been here a day!" I exclaimed.

"Try not to be hard on her, sugar. She's just trying to be motherly," Savannah said, looking at her watch. "But actually you're right. We should head over to work. I'm going to have you work with Beau in the box office tonight."

Before I had time to even rest for a second after running around the city with Joey, I found myself walking with Savannah to the theater. She said that some nights it was easier to walk than to deal with the traffic in the Quarter. On the way there, we passed some of the gay bars, and I couldn't help but peek in and look at the guys sitting on the barstools, some of them watching videos on large televisions. Sitting at a bar at four in the afternoon! I couldn't even imagine! One thing I did know was that before the night was over I was going to make it to one of those bars so I could get some firsthand knowledge of what the gay nightlife was like here.

*What an education I got that night.*

# CHAPTER 11

"Always make sure and double check the traveler's checks. We've gotten a few fake ones lately," Beau said.

He was prepping me on everything there was to know about working at the box office. Aunt Savannah told me I would be spending most of my time there helping out Beau. Of course, I'd rather be working with Joey, not that I complained though. Anything was better than being stuck in Andrew Springs at that moment.

"Any questions?" Beau asked. He drummed his fingers on the counter.

To be honest, I wasn't too sure if he was happy or not to have my help. He proved very hard to read.

"I think I've got it," I answered.

"Good, just make sure and ask any questions you might have. It's better to ask than to screw up and be stuck here until two a.m. trying to balance the receipts for the night."

"Gotcha. I think I'm good to go."

*I couldn't remember half of what he told me.*

Beau checked his watch.

"Looks like we have a few more minutes," he said. "So have you had a chance to check out the clubs?"

"Uh, not yet."

"Well, you're not missing that much. I feel like I've done it all…twice."

He got up and started straightening the pens, paper clips, and such. I started to follow suit. I wanted to prove myself a big help, or else otherwise I knew I might find my ass back in Andrew Springs scooping the mint chocolate chip.

"It looks like fun from what I've seen," I said. "Joey said that you and he go out together sometimes."

His face cracked a smile for the first time since he had been training me.

"Yeah, sometimes."

"Have you been friends long?" I asked.

"*Best friends*," he emphasized. "We've known each other for a little over two years. I met him about a year before he graduated from high school, after I moved down from Biloxi."

I thought about how nice it must have been just to have someone to come out with.

Beau opened up a side drawer and pulled out a pack of cigarettes. He lit one and took a long drag. His body seemed to relax as soon as he started smoking. He kicked back in a side chair and propped his feet up on the counter.

"We've had some wild times, Joey and me," he said.

"Wild times?" I said, raising an eyebrow.

Joey hadn't seemed too much like the wild times type.

"Honey, you can't be in this town and not have wild times. I mean, pleeeeeezzzzz," he said. He raised his eyebrow. "You'll know what I mean soon enough. You can count on that."

The wildest thing I had ever done was drink two beers within an hour at Bubba Joe's.

"Joey seems like a really nice guy," I said.

He took another long drag on his cigarette.

"Yeah, he's a really sweetie," he said softly.

He jumped up and stubbed out his half smoked cigarette.

"Well, I gotta take a piss before we open."

And with that he left me in the box office by myself.

My first night pretty much went without any major mishaps. I could feel Beau's eyes on me the whole time. He watched every step I made.

"Not bad for your first night," he said, still sounding a little skeptical.

I went searching for Joey afterwards. I hoped maybe he would go with me to one of the clubs, but Martha Washingtongue told me he had already left for the night.

I found Aunt Savannah and said to her that I wanted to go check out some clubs. She seemed hesitant to let me go out by myself, but I reminded her that I was out of high school.

"When I think about some of the things I did when I was your age," she said shivering. "Just promise me you'll be careful!"

"I'll just go out for a little while, and I won't wander off far until I know the city more," I said to reassure her.

She told me to have a good time, but I could tell that despite trying to be the "cool aunt" some maternal instincts were kicking in high gear. I'm sure she didn't want to deal with my mother if something did happen to me.

Then for the first time I went out on the streets of the French Quarter by myself. The streets seemed quite lively for a Tuesday night. Partygoers were making there way down Bourbon Street with huge frozen daiquiris in their hands, and I heard someone singing really bad karaoke from a bar across the street. I made my way through the crowd to the next block over, the corner of St. Anne and Bourbon. I knew exactly what I wanted to do, and that was to go to one of the gay bars.

On the left hand corner was a bar we had passed a few times. The doors around the building were wide open, and go-go boys were on top of the bar strutting their stuff for whomever might have a few extra one dollar bills or maybe more.

I noticed a lot of straight people who stumbled down the street would stop at the corner of St. Anne and Bourbon and peer into the bars at the goings on. They all had a look on their face that seemed to say that they could already tell that things were very different if you were to cross over to the next block of Bourbon. They would then abruptly turn around and head back in the direction of the other straight people to continue partying.

I took a deep breath and headed on into the bar. The place was packed with men and a few women for good measure. I also saw a couple of drag queens. I noticed a lot of eyes turn and look at me when I walked in which reminded me of Bubba Joe's, but that was one of the few things similar between the two. Bubba Joe's was never this packed or quite as lively. Some people sat on stools around the rectangular bar watching the strippers parading in front of them. Others stared ahead at the many televisions that played music videos, and some were in clusters of men talking, laughing, and checking out other men.

I first walked around the bar making my way completely around the rectangular bar. One of the bartenders screamed and threw a handful of napkins up into the air before breaking out into some random dance to the song "Love Is All Around." A few men, most of them older, smiled or winked at me as I walked by.

Shy, I would quickly avert my eyes and continue to try and push my way through the crowd, which took almost ten minutes. When I had finally checked out the whole place, I fought my way to the bar to try and get the bartender's attention. Within a minute, the bartender, a stocky, dark-haired guy, made his way over to me and slapped a napkin in front of me.

"What can I get you?" he yelled above the music.

At Bubba Joe's we just always bought our own drinks, which was usually cheap beer. I had no idea what I should order.

"Beer," I said.

The bartender winced.

*Didn't I realize that there were tons of different beers?*

"What kind?" the bartender said. He showed the irritation on his face since at least five other people waited to be served.

"Bud," I said.

I remembered that's what Houston always drank when he sat in the swing in the back yard reading the sports section of the newspaper.

The bartender scurried off and got my beer, and I paid him before he rushed off to take the next order.

I looked around feeling a little uncomfortable and not knowing what to do with myself. I looked up and saw a stripper shaking his ass in front of me. *Literally, his whole ass!* He only held a towel in front of his crotch area as he danced. I didn't know whether to stare, tip him, or move. So I just moved.

I saw a small spot in the corner had opened up next to the entrance to the bathroom, so I quickly made my way there. I sipped my beer and watched as people made the trek around and around the bar as if they might find something different each time they make the rounds.

Suddenly, I felt a hand on my butt. Then I felt the hand squeeze my butt! I froze not knowing what to do. Instead of moving, the hand stayed firmly planted on my ass.

I slowly turned around and came face to face with a man who was probably mid-forties and very tall. He had to have been at least six feet seven. He smiled at me revealing teeth that were an unreal shade of white. His hair was dyed a too dark black. When I looked down I saw he wore jeans that were so tight, if he farted, he would have probably busted a seam.

"You've got a nice little butt," he said, leaning down and mumbling into my ear.

I could smell the vodka on his breath.

Frozen still with fear, I just stood there. I wasn't sure how to deal with such a situation. I got the feeling he wasn't going anywhere if I didn't do something though.

"Uh, thanks," I said. I tried to walk away, but he put a powerful hand on my shoulder that stopped me dead in my tracks.

"You're funny," he slurred.

His other hand grabbed my ass again, and then it crept its way around to the front.

"I gotta go," I protested.

I tried to move away, but again he didn't let go. I looked around the bar and saw that everyone else was talking, watching the televisions, or downing their drinks. No one seemed to be noticing the panic that I felt sweep through me, and there was no one there to help.

I reached around and grabbed his hand and tried to pull it away from my body.

"No, thanks," I said sternly.

He looked at me with an irritated look. Obviously, he was not expecting this resistance.

"Come on, let me buy you another drink," he said. He tried to pull me with him toward the bar.

"No, thanks," I tried to protest.

Then I felt another hand on my other shoulder. This was a different person's hand, however.

"Norman, leave this poor boy alone. He don't want none of ya tired ass," I heard the voice say.

I turned around and saw Miss Althea from my aunt's theater. She was wearing a bright pink dress with white sparkles all over it. And at that moment this drag queen was my hero.

The tall guy turned around looking more irritated.

"Ain't nobody yanked your chain, Althea," Norman said.

With surprising strength Miss Althea lifted his hands from my body and shook her head.

"Just can't stop messin' with any of the new chicken that comes up in the coop," Miss Althea said, pulling me in the opposite direction.

The next thing I knew she led me to the opposite end of the bar where a table had just opened up. I grabbed one of the stools and so did she. I was so relieved at having been saved that I just sat in silence for a moment.

Miss Althea lit a cigarette and grunted.

"Um...um...um," she said.

"What?" I asked. I started to down my beer. I needed it about right then.

"Lesson numero uno, baby. Ya gotta be forceful with these mens around here. Sometimes they don't wanna listen, and you gotta be the one to make them. See that one over there," she said. She motioned in the direction of a white man who had to be in his seventies sitting on a stool and drinking out of a beer bottle.

"That one wanted to get all up into Miss Althea's stuff a few weeks ago, and I told him, I said, I don't think so. He tried his damnedest though. He sho' did."

"You knew that guy that was all over me?"

She laughed so loud that it was even above the music. A few people turned around and looked.

"Baby, Miss Althea knows everybody. She is the French Quarter. I've been cruising these bars since before you even probably crawled outta ya mama," she said. She patted her wig and then seemed to realize that she might have just dated herself. "But I was real young when I first started making an appearance."

"Who else do you know here?"

"Who don't I know?" she said.

She shook her head acting like this was some sort of challenge.

"What about the bartender?' I asked.

I motioned to the guy that had served me.

"Oh, baby," she said. She shook her head. "That there is a *saaaaadddd* story. That boy comes from one of the richest families in Memphis, but his family wasn't none too pleased when they found out he was strictly dickly. So they gave him a check and told him to ride his ass outta town. Well, he drank and snorted that check. Left with nothing, he started bartending here, and he done slept with half this bar, and the other half he just ain't met yet."

"What about...uh...her over there?" I asked.

I motioned to a drag queen that had jumped on the bar and was dancing with a very surprised stripper whose erect penis bobbed underneath the towel that covered it.

Miss Althea dramatically rolled her eyes.

"Oh, her..."

"You know her, too?" I asked, finishing up my beer.

"Um...hmmm...and she just wished she was half as fabulous as Miss Althea," she said. She eyed my empty plastic cup. "Now, baby, are we going to sit here and gossip all night or have some cocktails? Cause I know I need me a cocktail!"

She practically jumped off the barstool and went up to the bar. The bartender that practically tried to ignore me jumped to attention when he saw her. She then returned with a Long Island Ice Tea for herself and another beer for me.

"Thanks!" I said.

"Welcome to N' Awlins, baby," she said.

I took another look around the bar and motioned towards an older man that was standing next to the hallway leading to the bathroom.

"What about him?"

She laughed, and for the next hour or so she told me more stories about the various people around the bar. During that time, I finished the beer she bought for me and another one I bought for myself.

I felt a nice tingling sensation coursing through my body. Miss Althea's words and the beat of the dance music were starting to blend in together.

"Are you okay?" Miss Althea said. She stopped in the middle of her story about the muscular bald guy with the eagle tattoo on his arm that stood at the bar.

"Yeah, I'm cool," I slurred. "I gotta go pee though."

I stood up and realized that I couldn't feel my feet.

"Are you sure? Miss Althea's gettin' the vibe you could be a big old lightweight."

"Oh, yeah. I'm cool," I said.

I turned around and looked through the crowd for the hallway that I thought led to the bathroom.

I headed in that direction, and magically it seemed as if the crowd parted to let me walk through. In fact, it felt like I was floating through the bar. The beat of the music, the laughter, and the talking of the people echoed in my head. I had never felt this felt this kind of numbness and extreme relaxation.

And then I vomited.

Right there in front of God and everyone, I bent over and started hurling. It just seemed to come out of nowhere. My head felt like it was spinning, and those three beers came right back up.

I heard Miss Althea in the back shriek, "*Ooooohhhhh, no!*"

Then I felt her hand on my arm pulling me towards one of the exits.

*Not to the bathroom?*

"You need some air, honey. And you can throw up with all them other drunks in N' Awlins…in the streets!"

The heat and humidity of the August air hit me like a cast iron skillet upside my head, and I felt soooo dizzy. I leaned on the wall outside of the bar and looked at Miss Althea shaking her head at me.

"Honey, you a mess. You can hold as much liquor as a field mouse," she said.

"I'm going to be okay," I said, more to myself than her.

I had never felt so sick to my stomach or so dizzy. The skyline of the business district spun in the background.

I glanced back in the bar and saw some of the people inside staring at me with a look of disgust. I saw one of the bartenders heading towards the back with a mop. I couldn't remember when the last time I felt that embarrassed. I didn't know how it could get any worse.

Then I threw up again.

Miss Althea barely missed my vomit as I dropped to my knees and began to start heaving right there on the sidewalk.

*What a lightweight!*

"Oh, no!" Miss Althea exclaimed.

I heard some of the people in the bar go, "*Eeeewwwwwwww!*"

"Somebody had a little too much, huh?" I heard a familiar voice say above me.

I looked up and saw Joey staring down at me with those beautiful eyes that showed a mixture of pity and amusement.

It did get worse.

*Joey!*

*Ugh!!!!!!!*

"Hi," I said. I tried to stand up and play the whole thing off.

*Like an idiot.*

"You get him drunk, Miss Althea?" Joey asked smiling.

"Oh, no. Don't try puttin' this on Miss Althea. Don't be telling his auntie I did this to him! How was I to know he'd get so sick after just them few beers?"

"I'm okay. Really," I said. I stood back up and wiped my mouth on the back of my arm.

*Just lovely.*

"And what are you doin'?" Miss Althea asked Joey. "A fine boy like you should be out shaking yo' perky ass."

Joey blushed and smiled.

"A boy has to eat sooner or later, huh?" he said. He held up his bags of groceries from the Quarter A&P.

He then looked at me, and I could tell he was mulling something over in his mind.

"We should get you cleaned back up before you go home to your aunt's. She's likely to never let you go out again if she sees you right now. You should come back to my place for a few minutes," he said.

I didn't think Aunt Savannah would be one to get upset over this situation. In fact, she probably would have just been amused that I allowed myself to get so drunk and so sick. But I figured Joey was right that getting cleaned up first could be a good idea.

"Okay. Are you sure?" I asked. I felt sick again when I saw the trail of vomit I had left on the sidewalk.

"I was just heading home anyway," Joey said.

"Well, ya'll can go on, but Miss Althea's night has just begun," she said. She turned to me. "And, baby, promise me you won't drink so fast next time. The whole vomiting thing really won't help you land yourself a *huzzzband*."

"Deal," I said. I felt like shit cooked over a hot fire.

Miss Althea sashshayed back into the bar, leaving Joey and me behind.

"Are you sure?" I asked. "I'm probably not the best of company right now."

"Yeah, I'm sure," he said. He started to slowly walk down the street with me practically stumbling behind him. "You need some help?" he said, offering his arm.

The whole walk to Joey's I felt like my head would explode. Joey was telling me the story of one of the drag queens that had got into a very public fight with her very "married boyfriend" in the parking garage of the Montelone Hotel. He told it very matter-of-factly as if it were an everyday occurrence. I could only imagine what would happen back home if something such as that had happened. People would probably drop to their knees and begin praying.

Finally, we reached the 1100 block of Burgundy, and he led me up to a shotgun house, which were called such because each one had exactly the same layout. The first room was always the living room, then an open doorway lead to the bedroom, leading to an open doorway leading to the kitchen. You could shot a gun straight through the doorways, and it would travel through every room in the house, therefore, the name. This shotgun had seen its better days, but it still gave off a homey vibe with its plants and fresh coats of violet paint.

"Miss Althea lives in the one next door," he told me. He fished for his keys in his pockets.

"You've got to be kidding!" I said, sobering up.

"Nope, she's lived there for years," he said.

He opened the door and turned on the lights, and I followed him in.

The furnishings consisted of an overstuffed couch with a black slipcover along one wall, a small wood desk in the corner, a red rug in the middle of the room, and a small television across from the couch. The rest of the space was taken up with bookcases jammed packed with books. Many of the books were hardcover and looked worn and read many, many times. There were also a number of paperbacks. From the spines, it looked like a lot of them were sci-fi and also historical fiction.

"I'll be right back," he said, walking to the kitchen.

"Okay," I answered. My eyes roamed over the books on the shelves. "I'm going to clean up in your bathroom for a sec."

"Sure, you want coffee?" he called out.

"That'd be great, thanks," I answered.

My dizziness began to subside. I think the vomiting helped. I went into the bathroom, washed my face, and rinsed my mouth out. I was finally returning to normal.

I walked back into the living room and found Joey had taken off his shirt. He now wore just a form fitting white tank top that revealed that he some pretty decent biceps. I found myself doing a double take.

"Coffee will be ready in just a few minutes," he said.

"How come you didn't go out tonight?" he asked.

"Haven't really been in the mood lately," he answered. "I was kinda seeing someone for a little bit, and now I'm just kinda taking a break."

"Oh," I replied. I sat down on the couch when I started to feel a little weak.

"Always seems to be same thing…you know?" his voice trailed off. "What about you?"

"What about me?" I said laughing.

"Any great loves in your life?"

I must've blushed.

"Well, come on fill me in," he said.

I sat there in silence for a few seconds. The only boy I ever felt like I had any real feelings for was Billy, and I felt stupid telling him about my high school crush. He would probably just think it was silly.

"I'm sorry," he said, after a second. "You don't have to tell me anything. It's none of my business."

"No, it's no that," I said.

He sat down next to me on the couch and leaned back into the pillows.

"It's just that I feel like there's nothing really to tell…" I said.

"That's okay," he said. "You've got plenty of time,"

"Well, there was…" I said before I even realized it.

*Stupid!*

"I knew it!" he exclaimed. "There is a story!"

"Nah, it's nothing big."

I knew I had opened up a can worms, and there was no putting them back.

"There was this guy in high school…a friend of mine," I began.

"Sounds interesting so far…" he said.

"I have…had…a crush on him," I said. I felt sick at my stomach again.

I soooo wished that I hadn't brought this up.

"Straight? Huh?"

"Well…" I said, shaking my head.

"He's gay, too?"

"Well, I think maybe…Anyway, it doesn't matter. He's gone," I said.

"Gone where?"

"He left right after we graduated from high school for New York."

"Wow! That's pretty far!"

"Yeah…" I said quietly.

"Did you ever tell him how you felt?"

I laughed uncomfortably and began playing with the pillow next to me on the couch.

"I tried a few times. One time I actually thought I had," I answered.

He looked at me with a quizzical look.

"Long story, trust me."

He nodded and didn't push me.

"Well…I better check on the coffee," he said, getting up. "You want cream and sugar?"

"Yeah, thanks."

He headed back into the kitchen. I felt so sad thinking about Billy. I had spent most of the summer thinking about him, wondering about him, and longing for him, only to barely hear from him. He was starting a whole new life for himself, and maybe it was time finally for me to do the same.

Joey returned with the coffee. Its warmth alone seemed to make me feel better.

"Thanks," I said.

"Sure, no prob," he said. "By the time you go home I think you'll be fine. Just might want to take it a little easy on the brew next time."

"Ya don't have to worry about that. I learned my lesson about drinking."

*Famous last words!*

There was a weird moment of silence, and I decided to take the conversation into a completely different direction, anything to keep Billy from coming up again.

"You sure have a lot of books," I commented.

"Most of them were my mom's. She loved to read. Sometimes she would do it all day before she would go to work that evening. She'd sit at the kitchen table sipping chicory coffee and reading. She'd read just about anything she could get her hands on. When I moved here...after she passed..." his voice trailed off. "Well, I couldn't bring myself to get rid of them so I kept all of them."

"Looks like a lot of interesting stuff. You ever read any of it?" I asked.

"Yeah, not as much of it as I should. She used to tell me all the time I was just rotting my brain if I sat in front of the TV. Now that I'm thinking of going back to school, I think she might be right," he said. He got up and walked across the room where he picked up a small-framed photograph. "Here we are."

I looked at the picture in which Joey seemed to be around fifteen years old with a mop of curly, chestnut colored hair all over the place. His mother looked very young to have a son his age. She was a beautiful woman with perfect skin the color of dark mahogany and hazel eyes. Her hair was in cornrows and hung loosely around her smiling face.

"She was pretty," I said.

"Yeah, she was. She had a lot of men trying to date her, but she told me she had just given up on men, and that I was the only man that mattered in her life."

I didn't know what to say. I just sat there gulping my coffee. His voice was full of such sorrow and pain. I wanted to hug him right then and there I felt so bad for him. As much as my mom got on my nerves, I couldn't imagine her not being there anymore.

"Sorry, I didn't mean to get into all that," he said. He sat on the edge of the couch and straightened up the pillows on the couch.

"No, it's okay," I tried to say reassuringly.

"How you feeling?" he said.

"Better. I guess I better start heading back," I said, standing up.

"Okay…see ya tomorrow then," he said. He followed me to the door. "Hey, one thing…"

"Yeah?"

"Sorry about asking you all that stuff about your love life. I really shouldn't have…I was just…ya know…"

"It's no big deal. Like I said there's really nothing to speak of anyway."

"Okay. I do think your friend was the one that missed out though. You seem like a good guy. You do."

I was kind of taken aback by the compliment.

"Thanks," I said shyly.

I opened the door and stood in the doorway for a second.

"Thanks again for the coffee. Good night," I said.

"Night," he said.

He then stood there for a second looking like he wanted to say something. Instead, he wrapped his arms around me and gave me a tight hug.

His arms around me; I had to admit, felt pretty damn good.

"Maybe I should walk you back," he offered.

"No, no, really, I'll be fine."

*If I had only been thinking…*

"Are you sure?"

"Positive. See ya later."

I walked out and started to head down the street. I turned the corner, but I could have sworn in the corner of my eye I saw Joey watching me walk away.

# CHAPTER 12

❀

My time in New Orleans went by very quickly. I spent the time working in the theater box office and exploring the city, often with Joey. He seemed to really enjoy the company, and the more we got to know each other the more relaxed he became around me. Riding the streetcar down St. Charles Avenue was my favorite. We rode it all the way down to where it ended at Carrolton and ate at a place Joey swore had the best po-boys in town. He was right. They were good with tender roast beef covered in gravy.

The closer it got to the time for me to go home, the sadder I became. It was so freeing in the city. There was so much to see and do. All you had to do was hop on the streetcar or a bus, and you were there. New Orleans seemed to offer endless possibilities.

I also did my share of hanging out at the gay bars in the Quarter after work at the theater. I often went with Joey and Beau, who sometimes seemed a little miffed at the appearance of the third wheel. There just seemed to be a steady influx of new gay men everywhere I went. And, okay, I admit it. I got my share of looks, smiles, and hellos.

They were nothing compared to the ones Joey got. He would just sit in the corner nursing a beer. I saw many guys try to talk to him and flirt with him. He was never rude to them, but he always made it apparent that he wasn't interested. I couldn't understand why. I found myself wishing I got as much attention as he did.

One night I noticed a change in him though. He seemed to be laughing and smiling more when we would go to one of the local clubs. He also sort of started flirting back with some of the men that gave him attention.

Like Miss Althea, he also seemed to know a lot of people around the Quarter. Sitting at the bar many guys would come along and pat him on the back, give him a "Hey, baby," or a little peck on the cheek. I found myself getting a little jealous. But then I reminded myself that we were just friends, and he was probably out of my league.

"Drinks?" Joey asked.

I was sharing a table at the Pub with him and Beau late one Saturday after a particularly busy night at work.

"Rum and coke, sir," Beau said.

"I'll have a be…" I started to say.

Joey looked at the two empty glass bottles sitting on the table next to me.

"You'll have a water," he said, before leaving to try and make his way through the crowd to the bar.

I decided not to argue when I remembered my vomiting in the bar incident.

I caught Beau staring at me for a few seconds, and I began to feel uncomfortable. At times Beau was warm and friendly, and at others he acted like I was some huge burden he had to deal with.

"I can tell," he said, breaking the awkward silence between us that often appeared when it was just the two of us.

"Tell what?" I asked. I swayed my body to the beat of Madonna's "Erotica" playing in the background.

"Don't play coy with me," Beau said. He looked at Joey in the corner of his eye. "You've got a thing for Joey."

"Uh, what?" I mumbled, completely caught off-guard.

Was my developing crush becoming that noticeable?

Beau smiled slyly.

"I recognize that look, the one you have when you look at him," Beau said.

I glanced over to make sure Joey was still at the bar. The last thing I wanted was for Joey to overhear this conversation.

"I don't have a crush on Joey," I said. I failed to make eye contact with Beau as I spoke.

Beau chuckled.

"The hell you don't," he said.

I picked up on more than a hint of jealousy in his tone. That's when I realized where Beau's often indifferent or downright hostile attitude towards me came from. He also had feelings for Joey.

Before I could respond Joey placed two drinks on the table.

Sensing he had walked up in the middle of something from the strained looks on our faces he said, "What's going on?"

"Nothing," Beau said, lighting up another cigarette.

Joey looked at me, and I remained silent.

The next night at Aunt Savannah's theater, I sat in the box office counting the receipts for the night. Savannah walked in, kicked off her heels, and sat down next to me.

"Good night, Little Bit?" she asked.

"The best one this week," I answered, finishing up the counting.

"I sure am going to miss your help around here," she said. She reached over and tousled my hair.

"I'm going to miss being here," I said. "I'm going to miss it a lot."

"And Joey is going to miss you," she said. She nudged me in the side.

I wondered exactly what that meant.

*Clueless, yet again.*

"He's a good guy," I said.

I began putting the receipts away in the accounting files.

"Yes, he is, sug," she said. She stretched out her legs that were still in amazing shape for a woman her age.

I guess that's why she wore all of those short skirts.

"I wish I didn't have to go back," I said sighing.

"Aren't you excited about school?" she asked.

"Excited about going back there? No."

"I know your mom will be happy to have you back."

"But what if I'm not, Aunt Savannah? What if I'm not?" I said. I felt myself getting all depressed. "I don't think I want to go back."

"Oh, Lord! You're mother will kill me and you both if your butt isn't sitting in a classroom in a few days."

"Can you blame me? You know what I'm talking about, don't you?"

She nodded, but I could tell she was trying really hard not to sway me in the direction of staying.

"I feel so much freer here, ya know?"

"And what about school?"

"I can go somewhere around here once I get settled."

She shook her head. She knew that this would be drama.

"Look, Little Bit, I can understand where you are coming from. I've seen how you've become so alive while you've been here, but you have to think about your education, too."

"So you think I should go to school?"

"That's not what I'm saying. I just think you need to think about all of it really carefully before making any last minute decisions."

"I can't believe this is coming out of the mouth of the same Savannah who says living life on the edge is the only way!" I said.

"Shit, who knows? Maybe I'm getting old," she said shuddering.

"You? Never!"

"Well, God bless you for saying so! But seriously I will support you, whatever you decide."

"And would that mean that if I decide to stay here I can continue working at the theater?" I said. I tried to give her my best puppy dog eyes.

"Oh, your mother is going to kill me! Yes!" she said, throwing her hands up. "You can continue working here if you would like."

I shrieked in joy and threw my arms around her and gave her a big hug.

"Auntie's hair, baby! Auntie's hair! This is tomorrow hair, you know?" she said.

She fluffed up the hair I had managed to squash down in my excitement.

"Just promise me that you'll at least think about it overnight."

"Okay, okay, I will," I agreed even though I knew I had already made up my mind, despite the fact that I knew my mother's head would spin when I told her.

She reached down, gathered up her shoes, and then stood up.

"I'm going to go see if everyone has cleared out," she said, heading out the door.

"Aunt Savannah?"

"Yes?"

"When you said earlier that Joey was going to miss me what did you mean by that?"

"That he has a crush on you," she said.

She grinned and then walked out.

The next morning I knew it had to be done, but I dreaded it with everything in me. I picked up the phone, dialed the number, and after a couple of rings she picked up.

"Hello," Mother answered.

I took a deep breath.

"Hey, Mother," I said.

"I was wondering when I would hear from you," she said.

"You were?"

"It's almost time for you to come home, and I figured you'd want us to pick you up soon. You've got a lot of things to do before school starts next week."

"Yeah, Mother…uh…"

"Remember you have to get your books…"

"I'm not going!" I blurted out.

I knew I had to do it that way, or I may never get it out.

There was silence on the other end for a couple of seconds.

"Come again?" she said flatly.

"I'm not starting school this fall," I said firmly, even though my stomach felt like it was flipping.

"Of course you are. You got that scholarship. You are going to the college."

"It's just not the best thing for me right now," I said, trying to stand my ground.

"Mason, don't be stupid. Your father and I are not going to let you do this."

"You don't have a choice. I'm staying here, in New Orleans."

"Oh and just how do you plan on supporting yourself?"

"Aunt Savannah has offered me a job."

"Savannah!"

"Now before you jump all over her, I want you to know that this was my choice, and it was not her idea. She actually tried to talk me out of it."

"This is crazy, Mason!"

"Don't say that!"

"You're throwing away your chance for an education so you can spend time with all those sinners there! The men dressing up like women! All those homosexuals!"

With the last comment she might as well have slapped me across my face. I wanted to say, "You mean like your son?"

"The crime, the drinking…" she went on and on.

Now I was pissed.

"I told you, mother, I'm staying here whether you like it or not. I'm eighteen, and there's not a damn thing you can do about it!" I exclaimed. I had cursed at her for the first time in my life.

"Fine! Do what you want! But don't expect any help from us. You're on your own, Mason. You're on your own!"

And with that she slammed down the phone.

I tried to hold back a few tears that were beginning to form in my eyes, but I couldn't help it. I found myself crying for the first time since I was a kid. I knew though that somehow I did the right thing here.

I did what I needed to do for me.

A few days went by, and I began to settle into my new job. I enjoyed it. I felt so free and independent now that I knew that I wasn't going back to Andrew Springs. Everyone at the theater, except maybe Beau, seemed happy that I stuck around. All of the drag queens gave me hugs when they found out.

"We can always use some more eye candy up in here!" Suzanne Sugarcane said to me one night right before she went on stage to do a number of "Big Spender."

I stood backstage and watched her number since we had closed the box office a half an hour earlier. Across the way backstage, I saw Joey fiddling with the light board as he turned on a spotlight for her.

He smiled at me, and I felt an instant erection pop up in my pants.

*Hey, I was eighteen!*

I had thought a lot about my aunt's comment that she thought Joey had a crush on me. Sometimes I liked to believe that maybe it was actually true. Then sometimes I wondered if maybe it was just wishful thinking on her part. After all, if Joey had a crush on me, why hadn't he made any sort of move?

But I hadn't either.

We had continued to spend time together, and I even helped him with the math he studied for a college entrance exam. He hoped to start school in the next spring. He said he would start part-time and take classes during the day while he worked at night. I admired him for being so determined when he seemed to have had so many obstacles. I couldn't help but feel a little guilty. I did, after all, turn down a free ride to go to college, and he had to struggle.

One night when I was at his apartment, I was trying to remember everything I had learned in geometry the previous year, and our hands touched as we both tried to turn a page in the book at the same time. Our eyes met, and for a moment I wondered if it was true. Was he developing feelings for me, too?

After the show that night, he met me at the box office just as I was locking up. He had a mischievous grin that made him look even sexier.

"Are you ready?" he asked.

"For what?"

He walked over and grabbed me by the arm.

"We're going out! You can't be in New Orleans on Labor Day weekend, be gay, and not take part in Southern Decadence."

Joey had previously told me about Southern Decadence, and I had begun to notice advertisements for it in the gay part of the French Quarter weeks earlier. Joey and the drag queens at the theater had been telling me how wild the weekend would be.

"More cock than you could ever dream of!" Suzanne Sugarcane had enthused.

I heard stories that made the usual nights in the Quarter sound as holy as mass on Sunday mornings at the St. Louis Cathedral. Supposedly, the bars and the streets were so packed you could barely move, and all of that closeness ended up in a lot of naughty behavior. Miss Althea told me she had seen many a blowjob in the street, during the day, at Decadence.

Decadence happened every Labor Day weekend, and was referred to by many as the "gay" Mardi Gras. During the weekend, a parade was held by a huge group of people who met at a bar called The Golden Lantern. From there they went to every single gay bar in the Quarter with everyone drinking the whole time-as if the people in New Orleans ever seemed to need an excuse to drink.

As soon as we made it to Bourbon Street, I could already see that the streets were getting crazy on the Friday night of the Labor Day weekend. People weren't wasting a single second that they could be partying.

"This is nuts!" I said to Joey.

He grabbed my hand and began to pull me through the crowd.

"You ain't seen nothing yet!" he yelled back at me.

Many people were wearing beads just like at Mardi Gras. I glanced up at the balconies of the two bars on the corner of St. Anne and Bourbon, and they too were packed. Men were leaning over the balcony dangling beads and chanting, "Show your dick! Show your dick!"

And people were!

A few "straight" college guys intrigued by what was going on seemed to have wandered past the invisible wall. I saw a few of them giving in to the Show Your Dick Brigade. Oddly enough, they seemed to be getting off on waving their dicks around for these gay men.

"How are people getting away with this stuff?" I asked Joey when he pulled me off to the side outside Lafitte's bar where the crowd had not completely taken over yet. "I can't believe the police aren't arresting them!"

"The police have bigger things in this city to worry about for the most part," he said. "Plus, I think they turn a blind eye to a lot of the cock waving and sucking. They know that's why a lot of people come here, and they spend a helluva lot of money while they're here."

I could only imagine what would happen in Andrew Springs if people started chanting "show your dick." The old ladies would pass out, the police couldn't arrest fast enough, and the ministers would drop to their knees and start praying. Here people seemed to be dropping to their knees for other reasons.

"You look a little overwhelmed!" Joey said.

I glanced down and realized that he was still holding my hand.

*Still!*

"I thought I had already seen some wild stuff!" I said.

"Just wait," Joey said.

In the background between all the music and the yelling I thought I heard a familiar voice screaming out, "Miss Girl, up here!"

I glanced. Surprised, I saw Daniel hanging over one of the balconies. His hair was even a brighter blond than usual; he was wearing the shortest cut-off shorts I had ever seen. They were so short that I was surprised that his pubes weren't sticking out. And around his neck was a pile of plastic beads of all kind, some very large and extravagant. I already had an idea that Daniel had been a very "bad" boy.

He motioned for me to come up, and then he disappeared back into the crowd on the balcony.

"Who was that?" Joey asked.

"An old friend of mine from back home," I said. "Let's go up."

I led the way into Lafitte's Bar with Joey right behind me. I could feel his hand on my shoulder holding on so he wouldn't get separated from me. It seemed even more packed inside the bar than the street outside, if that was possible. I saw a few men wearing leather chaps and not much else. A stripper on top of the bar twirled his penis like a helicopter blade, and a bartender, yelling, threw a handful of napkins in the air littering the whole bar.

After careful navigation through the sea of horny men, we finally made our way to the staircase leading upstairs. I noticed on the way up the stairs that someone had already vomited on their way down-or way up. The smell was almost overwhelming.

When we finally made it upstairs, I turned around to make sure that Joey was still, indeed, behind me. He was, and he wrinkled his nose. I assumed it was because of the strong odor in the air-a mix of sweat and vomit.

"Do you see your friend?" he said. He had to yell right into my ear for me to hear him above the music.

I shrugged my shoulders and shook my head no. A second later I spotted Daniel just a few feet away. He was drinking his cocktail while some thirty-something guy had his hand down Daniel's pants, checking out his package.

When Daniel saw me he smiled, he casually removed the man's hand from his pants as if nothing more had been going on than a handshake. Out of the corner of my eye, I looked at Joey to read his reaction. I didn't want him to think badly of me as a result of what one of my friends was doing. He seemed unfazed though as he swayed his body to the music.

Daniel threw his arms around me and shrieked in delight.

"I was looking down off of the balcony, and when I saw you I said to myself, oh, no, she's not here, too!" he said laughing.

"I'm living with my aunt," I said practically screaming to be heard. "What are you doing here?"

"I came for Decadence, baby! I heard about it through some friends at school, and I just knew that I had to come. And come I have!" he said. He burst out laughing at his own pun.

"This is my friend, Joey," I said.

Joey held out his hand to be shaken.

"Hey," Joey said.

Daniel shook his hand, and he made no attempt to be subtle about checking him out.

"Joey," Daniel said. His eyes drifted down and then back up. "Nice to meet you."

He turned back and looked at me with a devilish grin. He then leaned over and said in my ear, "Where did you find this one? He's cute!"

I felt myself turn red, and Joey looked at me with a curious look since due to all of the noise he had no idea what Daniel said. At least I think he didn't.

"I work with Joey at my aunt's theater," I offered. I noticed that Daniel's eyes weren't leaving Joey's body.

Joey wore faded jeans and a black wife beater t-shirt which showed off his biceps nicely.

I couldn't help but find myself getting a little jealous. Even though I had yet to make my move, I cringed when anyone else hit on him.

"Are you from here?" Daniel asked Joey, before slugging back his cocktail.

"Born and raised," Joey answered.

"Well…I bet you have some Decadence stories then, don't you?"

Joey just smiled and said, "Maybe."

"So you got any dick yet?" Daniel said.

He sounded like he had asked me if I had seen any good movies lately, and again, I felt myself turn red.

"Daniel!" I said, play slapping him.

"All summer me and Ms. Thang here would go out to this tired gay bar in the middle of nowhere, and not once, not once, did she get her some. True they were all rednecks, but there were some that were kinda hot in a pick-up truck and hound dog kinda way. She got a lot of attention to…and not once," Daniel said. He shook his head like this was one of the world's worst tragedies.

Joey looked at me sympathetically. He could tell I was embarrassed. At least that's why I think he was looking at me sympathetically.

"I just haven't been ready yet! That's all! Is that a crime?"

"No, it's not," Joey said reassuringly.

I could tell he became a little amused by the situation.

I felt one of the guys in chaps grab my ass as he walked by. Startled, I jumped.

Daniel laughed, and Joey tried to suppress his laugh.

I began to feel a little self-conscious about my lack of experience. Was I really that far behind everyone else? Was I too much of a prude? Should I be going out getting laid all the time? Could Joey be scared to hit on me do to my inexperience? Do I overanalyze?

*Yes.*

"Where are you staying?" I asked. I had to yell louder than usual since a remix of "It's Raining Men" played even louder than usual.

Daniel gave me a quizzical look.

"Staying?" he asked.

"Hotel?" I said.

"Oh," Daniel laughed. He fingered his beads and checked out an older man who wore flannel on the end of the bar. "I don't have a place. I'm planning on working for my lodging the whole weekend. If you know what I mean!"

He burst out laughing and headed to the bar to order another cocktail. I wondered what Joey must think of me to have a friend like Daniel. Yeah, I thought he was kind of cool. Okay, I admit that I was a little envious of his sexual freedom, too. But sometimes he could come on a little strong. To say the least!

"Are you doing okay?" I asked Joey.

"Yeah, I'm cool," he said. His eyes wandered all over the room.

From the light off of the television playing videos, I could see again how beautiful his eyes were. I could get lost in them. I was definitely developing a full-blown crush.

He placed his hand on my shoulder and leaned towards my ear. "It's perfectly fine you know."

"What is?"

"You shouldn't do anything with a guy until you feel ready. Everybody is different."

"Ya think?"

"I know. Trust me," he said. "I'll go get us some drinks."

He made his way to the bar about the time that Daniel was back.

"This place is so fucking wild!" he squealed. "The guy at the bar asked if he could suck my dick. Right there!"

My eyes stayed on Joey though. What was I waiting on? Why was I so afraid?

"You've got it bad, don't you?" Daniel said nudging me.

"What do you mean?"

"Mary, don't you play dumb with me! You've got a thing for that guy bigger than fucking Montana, and you know it! And I bet you haven't done a damn thing about it, have you?"

I shook my head.

"You wait too long you're going to lose you chance. I guarantee you that one. Listen to me, Mary. I've been there."

That's when I saw Beau walk up to Joey and playfully put his arm around him.

If not Beau, someone was going to grab Joey up. I decided that it was going to be me.

Later in the night, Daniel found a law student from Tulane. He had bright red hair, freckles, and a washboard stomach. Daniel said he was taking off and that they were going to go "hang out", and he'd look for me later in the weekend. I never saw him after that. I guess things with the redhead went well.

Joey insisted on walking me back because I had managed to get myself a little lightheaded. Not vomiting all over the street, like before, but definitely more than buzzed. I couldn't believe it was almost four a.m. The streets were still packed.

We walked back to Savannah's, and I started to stumble a little bit on the sidewalk.

"Whoa!" Joey said. He put his arm around me. "Damn, you sure are a lightweight!"

Walking down Bourbon with his arm around me was definitely a rush. I figured some of the other partygoers thought we were together, and I liked that feeling. I felt so much safer with his strong arm around me.

"So how come you don't have a boyfriend?" I sort of slurred.

He laughed, and I could have sworn he pulled me in tighter as we walked, our pace slowing.

"I guess the right guy hasn't asked me out yet," he said.

"But you're so damn cute!" I said.

*Alcohol-the number one truth serum.*

We walked by a drunken old guy wearing a LSU sweatshirt who sat in the doorway of someone's house singing the country song "All My Exes Live in Texas." I was glad for the distraction because I couldn't believe what I just said. Yeah, I thought it, but I normally would never have the nerve to just come out and say it.

As we neared Savannah's, Joey said, "Wow, so you think I'm cute, huh?"

I felt myself beginning to sober very fast. My drunken mind went into overtime trying to figure out what would be the proper response.

"Well, yeah. I see guys hit on you or check you out all of the time when we're out, but you don't seem to do anything about it."

"I guess…" he started to say. We stopped outside the door that led to Savannah's. "I've been thinking a lot lately. Clearing my head I guess you could say."

Clearing my head? I tried to decipher that one, but I wasn't sure what it meant. Why couldn't guys just say what they mean?

*Funny, coming from me!*

"Oh, okay," I said. I dug into my pocket for my key.

"But, I…" he started to say. He shuffled his feet on the sidewalk.

"Yeah?"

"You're pretty cute yourself," he said.

I can only imagine how many shades of red I must've turned. I was so damn transparent sometimes.

"Really?" I said.

*Why couldn't you just say thanks?!*

"Yeah, I do," he said, looking me straight in the eye.

Finally, I said, "Thanks."

We had another little awkward moment. We both seemed to be waiting for the other to say something first.

At last he put his arms around me, and gave me another tight hug-one that lingered for a moment. His arms wrapped around me again made me want to melt. He stepped back, our eyes met, and I found myself getting lost once again in his eyes.

"I guess I better go in…" I started to say.

But then he pulled me closer to him and he kissed me gently, on the lips at first, but then more passionately. I felt myself relaxing as my lips parted, and his tongue slowly entered my mouth caressing mine. I wrapped my arms around him and returned his tight embrace-feeling the muscles along his back.

*It was freaking electric!*

When he pulled away, I took a moment to compose myself, and he reached down and took my hand.

"I'll let you go get some rest. Maybe we can talk about all of this later," he said.

"Oh, yeah. Sure. You bet," I said, sounding like a dork.

He gave me one last peck on the cheek, and he watched me open the door.

"Night," I said.

"Good night," he said before he started to walk away.

I shut the door to the courtyard behind me, and then I fell back against the door. I was in sheer heaven! Savannah was right! He did like me! Little Mason Hamilton from small town Mississippi had maybe just found himself a man!

I walked into Savannah's and tried to be as quiet as possible. I didn't want to wake her. I just wanted to go to bed and bask in the glory of having Joey give me a kiss. As I tiptoed towards my room, I heard the sounds of Dolly Parton's voice in "Steel Magnolias" saying, "That which doesn't kill us only makes us stronger."

I couldn't believe Savannah was still up. She always said eight hours of sleep was the key to looking fabulous in the long run.

The door to her room was open. So, I peeked in and found her sitting in the oak rocking chair she kept neck to her bed. She had a quilt wrapped around her that I remembered my mother had made for her many years ago out of pieces of their old clothes from when they were children. She had a pint of hazelnut ice cream in her hands. That's when I knew something must be wrong. Savannah always ate ice cream when she was depressed, and hazelnut meant that it was really bad.

"Aunt Savannah?" I said as I walked in.

She looked up, startled for a second, and then she smiled.

"Did you have fun, Little Bit?"

"Yeah. I ran into a friend from Mississippi."

"That's nice," she said faintly.

"Have you been crying?" I asked. I sat next to her on the bed.

"Shelby just told them she's pregnant," she said, referring to the movie.

Somehow I knew it was more.

"Why are you watching "Steel Magnolias" at four in the morning?" I asked. I pulled another quilt off her bed and wrapped it around myself.

"Guess I was just having trouble sleeping," she said. "Joey showed you a good time?"

"He kissed me," I said. I felt a rush of excitement flood through my entire body just by saying it.

Her face lit up.

"I told you!" she said. She slapped her knee. "I know new love when I see it."

"Well, let's not get ahead of ourselves," I said. "But it was very nice."

"He's a good boy, that Joey. Always has been. Always tried to take care of his mama from the time he was just a little boy. Did so right up until the end. He's seemed so much happier since you've been around. More than I've seen him in a long time."

I couldn't help but smile.

"What about you?" I asked.

"About me?"

"You're pretty, smart, a businesswoman. Instead of just trying to get others together, why don't you have a man?"

"Ah, I think that part of my life is over. Ever since my husband died…"

She rarely spoke about the man that she had married years ago who died soon thereafter.

"You were very much in love?"

"He was a good man. He loved me dearly. I was never in love with him; however, I never regretted the time I spent with him. He was a great inspiration."

"Surely, Savannah, you must have had some great love in her life," I said.

"Oh, yes," she said, her voice full of sorrow.

"Who was he?" I asked. I scooted to the edge of the bed to be closer to her.

"His name was Jefferson Crosby," she said. Her eyes lit up at the thought of him.

For some reason the name sounded familiar to me.

"Was he from Andrew Springs?"

"Yes. We fell in love in high school. He was so handsome, Little Bit, so handsome. He was tall with hair the color of corn silk and eyes the color of the blooms of an African violet."

"He sounds hot!" I said.

"Yes, hot," she laughed. "He was so sweet. He used to leave love notes right outside my bedroom window in the middle of the night. On the summer mornings when I would wake up and open my bedroom window, I would find them there waiting for me."

"Wow, that's so romantic!" I said dreamily. "So what happened? Tell me more!"

A look of sorrow swept over her face, and she seemed to be distant all of a sudden.

"Aunt Savannah?"

She turned to me finally and sat her ice cream on the night stand.

"You know that I left home at a very early age?"

"Yes."

"Did your mother ever tell you why?"

"No, but I always did kind of wonder."

"I left because of a broken heart. I left because my parents were ashamed of me, and I couldn't stand their looks of scorn anymore. I left because I felt like I had no choice if I wanted a decent life for me and my baby."

*Baby*! The word seemed to echo when she said it. I had no idea about any baby.

"What do you mean baby?" I asked.

"The summer before my junior year of high school I became pregnant with Jefferson's baby."

"I had no idea you ever had a child!" I exclaimed.

She reached over and patted my knee again.

"I know. It's not something that is spoken of."

"What happened to the baby? What happened with Jefferson?"

"The baby was conceived the very first time I ever made love. It was the night before Jefferson was to leave to go spend a few weeks during the summer with some relatives in South Carolina. I was all sad about him leaving. He said he had to go. He was going to spend some time learning his uncle's business.

His uncle was a banker or something of the sort. He said he could probably get a good job right out of high school, and then we could get married and move to Charleston," she said, sighing. "He took me out to the lake, the one over by where they have the county fair every year, in the brand new Thunderbird his father had just bought him. And that's where it happened."

"Then what?"

Obviously trying to come up with the words, she fiddled with the quilt for a moment.

"Well, Jefferson went to his relatives, and a few weeks later I started feeling sick. I was so naive at the time it never even crossed my mind that I could be pregnant. I had thought we had taken the proper precautions. And of all people, it was his father that told me."

That's when I realized why the name sounded so familiar to me. Dr. Jefferson Crosby, Sr. was a doctor in Andrew Springs who had been around ever since my mother was a little girl.

"Whoa! He was your doctor?"

She nodded her head.

"Yep, you got it right. Well, it didn't take the good doctor long to put two and two together to come up with a baby. Jefferson never even came back to town, and I never heard from him."

"That's awful. You never heard from him at all?"

"I just heard through the grapevine that his father had sent him off to some military school. Seems his son having a child with a girl from the other side of the tracks was not part of his plan. I don't know what his father told him that made him never contact me," she said. She shrugged her shoulders. "I just can't allow myself to believe that he knew about me, that he knew about our baby, and didn't even contact me."

"So what did you do?"

"Well, your grandparents were furious with me. They never were the most tolerant or loving of parents," she said. She ran her hands over the quilt. "I was embarrassed, I was heartbroken, a teenager, and pregnant. So in a moment of desperation I knew where your grandmother kept a wad of money in a coffee can in the kitchen. I stole that money, bought myself a bus ticket, and I came to New Orleans."

My eyes grew wide.

"And then?" I asked.

"And once I got here I was pretty overwhelmed, as you can imagine. I had barely been out of Andrew Springs, and here I was in some town I didn't know, sixteen years old, and pregnant."

"That had to have been so scary," I said, shaking my head.

"It was, but I was determined that I was not going back home. In desperation, I wandered into one of the Catholic churches here. I found a young priest, couldn't have been more than twenty-five, and I broke down right there in front of him. I can only imagine what a mess I must have looked like crying and carrying on. He made a couple of calls, and before I knew it, I was living at a house with a few other girls who had gotten themselves in trouble. I was told I could stay there until the baby was born, and the church would take care of me. After the baby was born, I gave her up for adoption to a family that social services selected. I only got to see her once for one brief second before they took her away."

"I'm so sorry," I said.

I remembered that night I found Savannah crying to my mother, and finally, it made sense.

"I then lied about my age and got a job as a cocktail waitress where they paid me under the table. Not too long after that my husband, Riley, came into the bar one night, and the rest…"

I put my hand on her shoulder.

"I'm so sorry," I said again. I didn't know what else to say. "Do you know what happened to your daughter?"

"No, the nuns told me it was for the best, and I think it was. After all, what kind of life could I have given her at the time?"

She reached over and picked up the remote control from the night stand and turned off the TV and VCR.

"Sometimes I just think about things that maybe I could've done different, but I have many blessings, many blessings in my life…like you."

When I woke up the next morning, or afternoon rather, I smelled chicory coffee and fresh biscuits. Savannah always made chicory coffee and buttermilk biscuits on Saturday when she woke up. She usually spent the first few hours of the day drinking her coffee, eating biscuits drenched in butter and honey, and reading her latest trashy novel. This week it was *Lust in the Laguna*. She said she needed that time to clear her head before Saturday's show, since Saturday was always the biggest night of the week.

I was still kinda shocked at her revelation from the previous night. In a way, a lot of things made sense now. Her relationship with my grandparents, why she left town, and the night I had observed her and my mother. Still, I wasn't sure if it was something I should mention or ever bring up in conversation again. It seemed to bring her great sadness, but yet I felt special that she shared that with me.

I wished that my aunt could find a special guy to have in her life. If anyone deserved it, I thought it was her. I wondered what was holding my aunt back.

I climbed out of my bed, reached down on the floor, picked up my pajama bottoms, and slid them on. The longer I smelt the coffee and biscuits, the hungrier I became. I couldn't believe it when I looked over at my alarm clock and saw that it was already past one. We would have to be leaving for work soon, and Joey wanted to go out to Decadence again tonight. I was happy to do it though if it meant I could spend more time with him, especially, if it meant I would get another kiss like I had the night before.

I went straight into the kitchen to grab some coffee. I was going to need some major caffeine to get going today. When I walked in, I was surprised when Savannah held out the phone to me.

"For you," she said.

My first thought was that it was Joey.

"For me?"

"Yeah, it's your friend Billy from back home," she said.

My heart skipped a beat. With all of the excitement with my new found feelings for Joey, I had finally begun to put some of my feelings for Billy in the back of my mind. So it only made sense he would call now! I couldn't believe he was calling me at Savannah's.

Savannah looked at me weird when I hesitated to take the phone, so I reached over and grabbed it. She raised an eyebrow. She knew there must be some sort of a story.

"Hello?" I said. The surprise was evident in my voice.

"Hey, Mace! What's up?" Billy said in usual Billy enthusiasm.

"I'm good. How's New York?"

"Oh, man, have I got stories!" he said. "When I called your house, your mom told me where you were staying. She sure as hell didn't sound very happy about it."

"She's not," I groaned.

"Good for you, man. Good for you. You shocked the shit out of me. I just knew you'd be starting school. Instead, you up and moved to New Orleans."

"It's been an interesting summer," I said. I wanted to imply that I had my own stories.

I walked out on the balcony and sat on one of the wicker chairs leaving Savannah and her trashy novel in the kitchen. My mind was being flooded with so many different emotions just by hearing the sound of his voice.

*Just when you think you've got some stuff settled, one phone call shoots it all to hell!*

"Well, I gotta big surprise for you," he said.

"You do?" I said. My mind spun out of control trying to guess what he could have to tell me.

"How about a visit from your best friend?"

"Are you serious?"

"No, I'm shitting you! Of course, I'm serious!"

"What about New York?"

"Oh, I'm coming back. I'll be in New Orleans in a few weeks, for a few days. I'm not coming alone..." his voice trailed off.

"You're not?"

I wondered who in the hell he could be bringing with him.

"Nah, a...friend...of mine is an actor, and he's coming down there to be in a special performance of a play for a few shows. So I'm tagging along for the hell of it. I already got the time off from the coffeehouse where I'm working. I'll have to take a lot of crappy shifts when I get back, but it'll be worth it."

"Oh, that's cool," I said, the suspense killing me. "Who's your friend?"

There were a few moments of silence on the other end, and I heard him clear his throat.

"Well, he's sort of my boyfriend," Billy said.

*Boyfriend!!!*

The word echoed in my head over and over.

*Boyfriend! Boyfriend?*

"Oh, that's cool..." I said.

*That's cool! That's all I could think to say to that statement?!*

"Yeah, his name is Steve. I think you'll like him a lot," he said.

*As much as you could like someone who was stealing away the boy you'd been in love with for years!*

"Boyfriend?" I said, still not getting over it.

"Well, yeah. Come on, Mace. You can't tell me that you're surprised," he said.

"No, I guess not," I said.

"I'm sure you've been having your own fun in the Big Easy," he said.

"What does that mean?" I said sounding testy.

"Nothing, Mace. Just you know…" he said.

"Yeah, guess I have," I said. I didn't know what the hell else to say.

I wanted to tell him about Joey. I wanted to tell him that I had found someone, too. But honestly I felt like someone had just stabbed me straight in the heart. As stupid as it might be, that's how I felt. After everything Billy and I had been through, why couldn't it be me? Why did he decide it should be this Steve guy?

*Steve!*

*Ugh.*

Right then and there, I decided that I hated the name Steve.

"Look, Mace, I gotta go right now, but I'll call you before we leave so we can hook up," he said.

"Great!" I said, trying to sound happy.

"I'm looking forward to seeing you," he said. He paused. I figured he waited for me to say the same.

"Yeah, me, too," I finally said.

"Bye."

"Bye."

I walked back into the kitchen where Savannah was beginning to do some cleaning up.

"Did you have a nice talk with your friend?" she asked.

"Full of surprises," I answered.

I felt like I could scream.

The next day, Joey went with me to do some shopping at the Maison Blanche department store on Canal Street. After getting a few paychecks from Aunt Savannah, I had a little extra money, and I decided to buy myself a few new clothes as a treat. I didn't have a very large wardrobe since a lot of my stuff was still back home. I couldn't keep wearing the same clothes out to the bars, could I? I had mentioned that I was going to Joey the night before, and I asked him if he would like to come along. Joey didn't seem like a guy too interested in shopping. His wardrobe seemed to consist of various color t-shirts and pairs of faded jeans. I did enjoy his company though, and he said he'd like to join me.

My mind had been doing double time trying to figure everything out from Joey's kiss to Billy's visit. I felt confused and conflicted about all of it.

"Do these look okay?" I said. I walked out of the dressing room in the young men's department. I was buying a new pair of jeans, and I never could figure out which fit was right for me. Boot cut, slim, baggy, relaxed…what the hell?

Joey sat in a chair outside the change room.

"Turn around," he said.

"What?' I asked.

"Turn around," he said.

I did a quick turn around and then looked at him for his reaction.

He smiled

"Just right," he said smiling.

I felt myself blush.

The sixtyish saleslady, who had probably been working there for forty years, tried to suppress a grin as she looked at Joey and back at me.

"Should I get you another size?" she asked. She scratched her scalp. Her hair was so stiff with hair spray the whole "do" moved when she scratched.

"I think these are okay. I want to look around a little more," I said.

"I'll hold them at the register for you," she offered, pushing her glasses up from the tip of her nose.

I went back into the dressing room and changed back into my old jeans. As soon as I walked out, the saleslady took them from me.

I walked around looking at the shirts with Joey behind me.

A vest! That's what I needed! I thought as I looked through a rack of multi-colored ones that were so bright they probably glowed in the dark.

"Did I embarrass you?" Joey asked.

"When?"

"When I told you how good the jeans looked in front of that lady."

"Of course not," I lied.

"Can I ask you another question?"

I stopped looking through the rack and turned to him.

"Sure."

"Why have you been so quiet lately?" he asked, with his arms folded.

The previous night I had gone out with Joey again to enjoy the Decadence festivities. We met up at Good Friends Bar on St. Anne with Miss Althea and Suzanne Sugarcane, who of course were in full drag. I wasn't sure if I would recognize them out of drag since I had never seen them that way.

We had a few drinks. I had a couple of Long Island Iced Teas. They were laughing, and Miss Althea grabbed a lot of stranger's butts as she walked around the upstairs balcony. All I could think of was Billy and his visit. And

Steve! *Steve!* How was I going to react when I saw them? Even though it was pretty damn obvious Billy and I had never officially came out to each other. And now he was showing up with a boyfriend! He had to have known I had a thing for him. Didn't he?

And there was Joey. Cute. Attentive. He planted a wallop of a kiss on me the night before, and all I could think about was Billy right then. He'd try and engage me in conversation, and I know I must have seen preoccupied. I even called it an early night, and when I said I was going home he looked very disappointed. Why couldn't I just forget about Billy?

"I've been quiet?" I asked, trying to play it off.

"Did I freak you out with the kiss?" he asked.

His eyes were full of genuine concern.

"No, the kiss was…it was…great!"

"I was wondering after last night. I was hoping maybe last night we would've…"

"Would've what?"

He paused, looked down, and shrugged his shoulders.

"Done it again," he said softly.

I felt so bad. The previous night Joey was hoping that things between us could progress, and I was all obsessed thinking about Billy. He must've felt rejected, especially when I went home early.

"I've just had some stuff on my mind lately, but none of it has to do with you. You're…well…great, Joey. I think you're wonderful."

"Really?" he said, looking a relieved.

*Did I feel like an ass or what?*

"I like you a lot," I said.

He took a quick look around the young men's section and saw only the saleslady putting those ink tags on jeans. He hesitated for a second, but then he placed a quick kiss on my lips.

I felt my whole body tingle, and for a moment I forgot all about…

Oh, yeah, Billy.

Afterwards, Joey went home to shower, and I went back to Savannah's. We decided we would meet at the Clover Grill, a dive diner in the heart of the gay district of the Quarter, for an early supper. I was determined that I was going to just focus that evening on this awesome guy, a guy I had thought was out of my league.

When I walked into Savannah's carrying my bags from Maison Blanche, I found her sitting on the edge of the couch as if she had been waiting for me.

"Hey! I got some really cute stuff. A lot of the summer stuff was on sale," I said, sitting down beside her.

I started to pull some of the stuff out of the bag, but when I looked up at her I saw it in her eyes. Something was wrong. Something was really wrong.

"What is it?" I asked. I felt my stomach clench in nervousness.

"Little Bit, you need to call your mother," she said quietly.

"Why?" I said, my voice rising in alarm.

She looked down at the floor and fidgeted with the hem on her skirt.

"What's wrong, Aunt Savannah? Tell me! Please!" I pleaded.

"It's Elvis. Your father had a heart attack."

# CHAPTER 13

I had never before felt so powerless as I looked at him. He slept while I sat in a chair next to the bed staring at him. He had always seemed so strong, so rough and tough. I hardly saw him so much as shed a tear. Who knows? Maybe that's why he was here now.

The only sound in the room was that of the heart monitor making its steady beeping sound. Mother and Cherie had left a few minutes earlier to go to the cafeteria. I didn't want anything to eat. I had had no appetite ever since Savannah told me the news.

It was true that my father and I had never been close. Actually, that's an understatement. I had always thought of him as someone who was clueless where I was concerned. We had never been able to relate about anything. The times he spoke the most to me were when I was usually in trouble, and he had to scold me. It was if he was a person who had always been around, but as I sat there I realized I wasn't sure who he was inside. He had never spoken of any of his dreams. Did he have any? I thought everybody must. I think he thought the showing of any emotion outside of anger was a sign of weakness. An unhealthy trait passed on by my grandfather, the stern of the stern.

I think he knew that I was somehow "different." In fact, I'm sure he knew on some level, but was unwilling to accept it completely, which is probably why he seemed especially distant to me. If he stayed away, maybe he could keep from having to deal with it.

A man's man had no idea how to deal with a queer as a son.

I noticed that with Cherie he had always seemed a lot closer. His face would light up a little more when she won her pageants. He used to take her out to father/daughter dinners at the Andrew Springs Steakhouse when she would win, just the two of them. He said it was their special time together.

Despite all of this, I found myself freaking out when I heard the news that he had had a heart attack. After all, he was my father. He had always been there in some sort of way. Did it make me think about my own mortality? Was it the fear of a little boy wondering if he would ever have any sort of connection with his father?

Cherie walked in carrying a cup of that harsh vending machine coffee.

"Thought maybe you might want this," she said, handing it to me.

"Thanks," I said. I took it from her, but I wasn't very eager to drink it. "Where's mother?"

"In the lounge watching the news. I think she needs to get her mind on something else for a little while."

Dad made a little snort in his sleep. Something he often did while he slept in the recliner in front of the television.

Cherie looked up at the heart monitor. I could see the fear in her eyes.

"The doctors said it was just a mild one, right?" I asked.

She nodded yes.

"This time. They said he'll have to start exercising and eating right."

I chuckled. My father's idea of exercising and eating right was walking to the kitchen to grab a bag of potato chips.

"I'm sure Mother will stay on his case," I said.

She pushed some stray hairs out of her face, and I could see the gray bags under her eyes. I don't think she had slept in almost forty-eight hours. Houston stayed at home and took care of the baby. He was probably trying to figure out how to heat a bottle and how to change a diaper that very moment.

"Mom's still pissed with me, huh? She's barely said three words to me since I've been here," I said.

"She was pretty ticked off when you didn't come home to go to school. She didn't talk about it much, but I knew that she was pissed."

"It's not her life though. It's mine," I protested.

"Why don't you go talk to her? I'll sit here with Dad."

I hesitated. I wasn't sure how ready I was to have this conversation with my mother. I was already stressed out enough.

"Go on," Cherie said. She nudged me with her elbow.

I reluctantly got up and went into the waiting room where Mother sat in front of the television, watched "Wheel of Fortune", and nervously played with the strap of the big, brown worn leather purse she must have had for years.

I walked in, and without saying anything to her, I sat down beside her. Her eyes never strayed from the television; however, so I was pretty lost trying to decide where I should begin.

"He's looking better," I said finally.

She sighed and replied, "Yes. Our prayers are being answered."

There were a couple of more moments of silence as I struggled to figure out what to say next. The only noise was the clapping contestants on the game show as they spun the wheel and chanted, *"Big money!"*

"Is it going to be this way the whole time I'm here?" I asked.

For the first time since I walked into the room her head turned, and her eyes met mine. I could see the anger brimming in them.

"Like what?" she asked.

"With us barely talking and you mad at me?"

"How do you expect me to be, Mason?"

"I don't know. I hate this though. I hate it."

"As hard as your father and I worked to raise you, to give you the things we never had, to give you an education, only for you to throw it all away. For what?"

I rubbed my temples. I felt a headache coming on.

"I need some time to figure out what I really want to do with myself."

She grunted and took a piece of gum out of her purse and popped it into her mouth without offering me any. It was my favorite brand, too. Juicy Fruit.

"And you have to do that in New Orleans, not here with your family?"

"I needed to get away from Andrew Springs for a while to see what else the world has to offer."

"Everything you need you have right here," she snapped. "What if your father would have died last night? You wouldn't have had time to make it into the hospital."

"Christ, Mother! I can't believe you said that!" I said. I felt my face flush from anger.

"Don't you use the Lord's name…"

"Fuck that! I can't believe what you just said to me! How can you be so cruel?" I said.

I felt tears beginning to form in my eyes.

But I never cry.

*Just like my father.*

I saw a nurse pop her head in to see what the commotion was about. She looked at mother and me, but we now sat in silence. Satisfied that the scene was over, she then walked on down the hall.

"You will never use that type of language around me again. Do you understand?" she said. She kept her eyes on the television while the contestant decided whether to spin again or buy a vowel.

"I have to be where I am…for now," I insisted.

"Have you been using that type of language ever since you moved there? Is that what that evil town has taught you?"

"You don't know anything about New Orleans, Mother. Like everyone here is so kind and understanding. That's why Aunt Savannah had to leave here, isn't it?"

She flashed me a look of surprise that said she wondered how much I knew, but she said nothing.

"That town is filled with alcoholics, murderers, and homosexuals!" she exclaimed.

I felt like someone had just slapped me across the face, stinging pain.

I had often wondered if my mother had come to any conclusions about me. After all, I was eighteen and I had hardly mentioned any girls. Yet, if she did have a clue, it made all of this even worse to me. It was like she was telling me what she thought of me, that I was along the same line as a murderer. A murderer!

I sat there and looked at my mother. Her eyes were red from lack of sleep, her arms were crossed, and she chewed her gum as if she were ripping it to shreds in her mouth. I had never felt so hurt in my entire life.

Determined that she wouldn't see me cry, I got up and began to walk away without even responding to her remark.

"Where are you going?" she demanded.

"As soon as we know for sure he's okay…I'm leaving. I'm outta here," I said, walking out.

I walked down what seemed like endless corridors, nurses and doctors, and hospital rooms. I felt my body tense up, but I wasn't going to do it there. If it was going to happen, I didn't want anyone to see me.

Finally, right when I felt like I couldn't hold it in much longer, I saw a sign pointing to a stairwell. I went through the door, and sat on the bottom step. And I cried. No, actually I sobbed. I buried my face in my hands, and I felt my whole body shudder with this outpour of emotion that had been kept so neatly, tucked away inside for so long.

I found myself crying about everything, not just my father, or what my mother had said that hurt me so much. I cried about Cherie looking so tired and worn out at the age of twenty. I cried over my not ever telling Sylvia the truth about myself. I knew that as a result I had distanced myself from her, too. I cried about Billy. I had wanted him for so long, only for him to find someone else in what seemed like an instant, even though I was convinced he must have known how I felt about him.

And when I finally felt like I had gotten a lot of it out, I leaned against the wall in the stairwell and just sat in the silence alone with the thoughts and emotions that I had run away from for so long.

*Running from as if my life depended on it.*

# CHAPTER 14

❀

The next couple of days few words were exchanged between my mother and me. I think that if she didn't have a clue before she certainly had one now after she saw how I had reacted to what she said. She showed me very little regard, and the hurt only deepened.

The day my father was released I asked Cherie to take me to the bus station. It was time to go back to New Orleans.

"You're going back already?" Cherie asked. She seemed genuinely disappointed.

Motherhood had seemed to bring out a lot of maternal instincts in her that I never knew she had. She often looked after me while I was there to make sure I ate, if I needed laundry done, and if I slept.

"Do you need a little nerve pill?" she asked. She unwrapped a crumpled tissue she had pulled out of her purse to reveal a small blue pill. "Dr. Peterson gave them to me when I freaked out a few weeks after the baby was born. They come in handy at a time like this."

"I think I'm okay," I said. I felt warmed by her concern and disturbed by her pill popping and drug pushing at the same time.

Cherie also noticed that things had only gotten worse between mother and me. I think she felt responsible because she was the one that pushed me to go talk to her at the hospital.

The baby, Lily, slept strapped into her baby seat in the back. I wondered what it must be like to be so at peace, for your biggest worry to be when you would get your bottle again. With her big brown eyes and curly reddish hair, she was beautiful. She had begun to steal my heart during my otherwise horrible visit. When she smiled at me while I fed her a bottle, I felt myself melt.

"What went down between you two? Why won't you tell me?" she asked, as she drove me to the bus station.

I wasn't sure how to respond to her question.

"I guess she's just still pissed with me about the school thing," I said.

I saw her biting on her lower lip, which I knew she did when she felt like she was being spoon fed bullshit. Kinda like the night before her wedding to Houston when he insisted that he only played poker with his buddies the night before.

But she said nothing more on the subject when she dropped me off at the station.

"Want me to wait with you?" she offered.

"Nah, I'll be all right," I said.

I got out of the car and grabbed my bag out of the backseat where it sat next to Lily. I gave Lily a little kiss on her forehead and told her to be a good girl for Uncle Mason. The only thing that made me feel kind of bad for leaving Andrew Springs again was that I knew I'd miss watching her continue to grow up.

"Bye!" Cherie yelled from the car.

She drove off home to cook dinner for everyone. Mother hadn't cooked in days.

I found myself relaxing as I boarded the bus for New Orleans. As we pulled out of the parking lot, I watched through the window as Andrew Springs went by until we were gone, and I left town once again.

When I got back to New Orleans, I told Savannah what had happened.

"Sometimes I can't even believe that she's my sister!" Savannah said.

She shook her head and clutched the ruby necklace around her neck.

I sat at the kitchen table with my head hung low picking at the mustard greens, corn bread, and fried catfish Savannah had fixed in a spontaneous burst of domestic urges.

She got up from her end of the table and walked over to me and put an arm around me.

"You know you have a home here with me as long as you need it," she said.

I smiled, but inside I was still hurting pretty badly after what happened.

Savannah must have said something to Joey, even though I'm not sure what, because he showed up that night on his day off intent on taking me out and showing me a nice time. He took me to dinner at a seafood place in the Quarter and ordered one of my all time favorites-an extra large shrimp po-boy.

After that, he took me to seem some sort of "art" film at the Canal Place Cinema. I can't remember the name of it now, so it must've not been that great. Or more likely, it was because my mind was still on things back home, my mother's anger, and my father's heart attack. Not to mention that in the back of my mind I knew that Billy would be showing up in New Orleans.

*Billy-with Steve.*

After the movie, we took our time walking down Decatur Street towards Jackson Square. The first taste of fall was in the air. It was an unusually cool evening for late September. Carriage drivers waited patiently outside Jackson Square for tourists eager to spend thirty dollars to ride through the Quarter and hear made up stories of it's past. A jazz band had set up right outside the beignet and coffee place, Cafe Du Monde. A small crowd had gathered around the band, and they were occasionally throwing dollar bills into a rusted coffee can.

We stood and watched the band play for a second. I tapped my foot in time with the music and hummed along.

"I play the sax," I said. "Well, use to play the sax."

Joey raised an eyebrow in surprise.

"No kidding?"

"Yeah, I even got a scholarship to go to college because of it. But as you can see I didn't take it."

"Regrets?" he asked.

We started our stroll down Decatur Street towards the Farmers Market.

"Sometimes...no...hell, I don't know," I said. "My mom was so pissed."

"How were things back home?" he asked.

I was silent for a moment as I stopped for a moment and stared into one of those tourist stores that sell the "voodoo" materials.

"I don't know," I said, shrugging my shoulders.

We continued walking along, and I felt him put a hand on my back.

"You don't have to talk about it if you don't want to," he said.

"No, it's okay. It's just my mom doesn't understand why I want to be here. It's like she takes it almost as an insult that I don't want to be in Andrew Springs. She also said something that kind of pissed me off...or hurt me, I guess."

We took a left turn down Governor Nichols, and I knew we were heading in the direction of Joey's place.

"What did she say?" he asked.

"She said she didn't understand why I would want to live here with all of the murderers, alcoholics, and homosexuals."

"Damn! What does she really think of the city?"

"Yeah, I know."

"I'm sorry."

"She just doesn't get me, and it pisses her off."

We took a left on Burgundy, and passed a homeless man who was begging for money as he sipped out of a brown paper bag. Joey fished the spare change out of his pocket and handed it to him.

"Have you thought about being straight up with her about your being gay?"

I shuddered at the thought.

*"My son a homosexual!" I could hear her shrieking.*

"She would just freak out. And my dad...oh, man."

"You don't think on some level she already knows?"

"Maybe."

"I'm not going to tell you what I think you should do one way or the other. I was worried about my mom, and she shocked the shit out of me by telling me she had known that since I was a little boy."

We made it to his shotgun apartment, and I followed right behind without questioning.

Just as he was putting his key in the lock, Miss Althea practically fell out of her front door.

"Girl, these heels are going to kill Miss Althea!" she said. She regained her balance and showed off her five-inch stiletto heels. "Just got'em today at the Five Dollar Shoe Warehouse in Mid-City. They look hot, but I ain't never worn any this high, honey."

Besides the bright pink heels, she wore a black mini-dress and a pink scarf around her neck, tied in a perfect bow.

"Where are you going Miss Althea?" I asked.

She raised her eyebrows.

"To see my *huzzzzband*," she replied.

Joey and I gave each other a quizzical look.

"Miss Althea's life don't just revolve around Miss Savannah and her house of performance, you know. I do have myself a love life...um...hmmm."

"Good for you," Joey said. "Everybody needs that."

She raised her eyebrows and looked at the two of us.

"I knew something would be goin' on between you two young bucks before it was over," she said grinning.

"Oh, really?" Joey said, nudging me.

"All of the girls at the theater notice how you two be lookin' at each other-all goo-goo eyes."

As always, I felt my face flush. I could only imagine what shade of red.

"Are you saying we've been the talk of the changing room?" Joey asked, smiling widely.

"You know it," she said.

She smoothed her dress down.

"Now I told ya'll Miss Althea was going to go see her *huzzband*. Ya can't hold me up no more!" she said. She walked down her steps and down the sidewalk with a loud *clop, clop, clop* of her heels.

Joey opened his door and motioned for me to come inside.

I walked in and plopped down on the couch.

"You want something to drink?" he asked.

"I'm okay," I answered.

And in a move that surprised even me, I grabbed Joey by the hand and pulled him down on the couch with me.

"Will you just lie here with me?" I asked.

Surprised, he smiled and nodded yes. He pulled me close to him and snuggled up to me. His arms around me, holding me tight, was just the comfort that I needed.

"I meant to tell you earlier," he said, whispering in my ear. "I passed my college entrance exam. I think I'm going to be able to start school in the spring."

"Joey, that's great!"

And then we kissed.

And then the next day Billy arrived…earlier than I expected.

# CHAPTER 15

It was a crazier night than usual at the theater. Three people on the staff called in sick. Not only was I going to have to man the box office before the show, but I'd also help out at the bar and help Joey manage the stage. Luckily, Joey had shown me a few steps on the lighting so I was able to help him out with that.

Things between us seemed to be progressing along fairly well. We took a bus the previous day to Biloxi where we hung out on the beach on one of the last days before summer. We were out practically the whole day, and I had the pinkish burnt skin to prove it. Joey, of course, had just turned a nice chestnut brown.

Towards the end of the show I stood on the sidelines and watched Martha Washingtongue sing "Somewhere Over the Rainbow" when I felt Joey's hands slide around my waist. He kissed my neck, and I felt like putty in his strong tawny hands.

"Hey, handsome," he whispered in my ear.

I turned around, and we gave each other a peck on the lips.

"Ah, young love. Reminds me of when I was a young, innocent girl," Suzanne Sugarcane said. She walked by and twirled the sash on her Oriental style robe with the fire breathing dragon stitched on it.

Both Joey and I giggled.

I nuzzled Joey's neck and almost forgot I had a light cue coming up soon.

"Maybe we can go get a quick drink after work," Joey said, looking all puppy-eyed.

*How could I resist?*

I heard the song about to end and quickly turned back around to the lighting.

The crowd was going wild with applause as Martha left the stage.

"See that guy in the front row wearing the blue polo," Joey said. He pointed to a handsome man, probably in his late forties, with salt and pepper hair and a rather built body.

"Who is he?" I asked.

"I saw him come by earlier today with flowers for Savannah!"

"Really!" I exclaimed. I tried to check him out more although the bright lights made it tough to see clearly.

"I heard him tell the bartender he was an old friend of hers," Joey said.

Savannah certainly hadn't mentioned any man who was showing her interest. But why wouldn't he? She certainly was still a very beautiful woman. I couldn't figure out how she was still single anyway. I had just come to the conclusion that she preferred it that way.

Savannah went out on the stage to thank the audience for coming and to throw out one last joke to get a laugh, something about Martha having bigger tits than her or something. She was wearing a knee length red dress that had a slit practically up to her waist, black heels, and charcoal stockings. Her hair was pulled back into a bun with just a few curly strands surrounding her face.

I noticed the man in the audience seemed captivated by her as he sipped his drink, probably whiskey-straight up. That was the kind of guy he looked like. I would have to ask Savannah for the scoop later.

As Savannah left the stage, I lowered the lights, and Joey lowered the curtain.

"Good job, girls!" Savannah called out to all of the drag queens backstage.

They ran around taking off costumes, wigs, and piles of make-up.

"You ready to go get that drink soon?" Joey asked.

"Sure," I said.

We began to walk offstage down to where the audience sat.

"Look what I found!" I heard Savannah call out from towards the front entrance.

I looked over and next to her stood Billy.

*Oh, shit!*

I stopped dead in my tracks and just stared at him, which must have been noticeable to Joey, whose eyes I felt on me. I'm sure he tried to figure out who stood next to Savannah.

"Hey, Mace!" Billy called out, waving wildly.

He looked taller. He looked more built. He looked blonder. Damn, he looked even cuter than the last time I saw him. And that famous Billy Harris smile gleamed at me all the way across the theater.

"Billy…" I muttered. I think I sounded more shocked than happy.

"Surprise! We got here early," he said. He started to walk towards me.

*We?*

*Yep, we.*

That's when I noticed the man walking behind him. And when I say man, I mean *man*. He had to have been at least thirty five, which meant he was old enough to be Billy's father. He had dark, wavy hair and a very light complexion, almost pasty, and he had what looked like a few days worth of stubble on his face. He was a few inches taller than Billy, and bigger. He was very built. You could see through the light blue t-shirt he wore his huge pecs and bulging biceps.

It was Steve.

*And I already hated him.*

"Isn't this a nice surprise!" Savannah exclaimed.

Billy and Steve walked up to Joey and me, and I saw Billy give Joey a quick once over. Billy grabbed me and gave me quick hug. Feeling his familiar arms around me again flooded me with so many different emotions. Even smelling his skin, always with that faint smell of that soap brand from Ireland, sent me back. I felt like that awkward sixteen-year old boy all over again, the same sixteen-year old boy that was hopelessly in love with his best friend.

"It's so great to see you, man!" Billy said. He slapped me on the arm in some weird display of masculinity after giving me the hug.

"You, too. I'm…glad to see you," I said.

He motioned Steve to come over.

"This is my boyfriend, Steve," he said. He beamed as Steve walked over and offered his hand to be shaken.

"I've heard a lot about you," Steve said in a very deep voice.

I have to admit I was pretty taken aback. While I expected Steve to be handsome, I didn't expect him to be from another generation!

I shook his hand and smiled meekly.

"Nice to meet you," I muttered.

For a second the four of us Billy, Steve, Joey, and I just stood there in some sort of an awkward moment. Here stood Billy, my closest friend for years, and I was so shocked I didn't know what to say.

Joey broke the silence when he shook both of their hands and said, "I'm Joey."

I felt like such an ass. I hadn't even introduced Joey.

"Nice meeting ya, Joey," Billy said. He looked him up and down, and then gave me a look as if he were trying to determine what my relationship was to Joey.

I caught Savannah's eye in the background. She could pick up on the fact that something was a little off about this whole reunion.

"Well," Savannah said. She walked over and placed an arm around me. "If you boys are hungry, I could sure use a bite. My treat! Billy, you and Steve must be starving after your long trip."

Billy looked at Steve for approval.

Steve smiled.

"That would be great," Billy said. "I can't wait to hear what you've been up to, Mace."

Billy and Steve began to follow Savannah out as she chatted away about how they had to come to one of her shows, and how she remembered meeting Billy for the first time. It was just after his family had moved into the neighborhood, and he had come over to hang out with me some on Christmas Eve afternoon. She spoke of what an amazing smile she thought he had even then.

I looked back at Joey who seemed to be hesitating.

"Billy is an old friend of mine from back home," I said.

Joey nodded.

I wondered if he knew that Billy was the boy I had spoken about, the one I told him I had been in love with.

"Maybe I should just let you catch up with your friend," he said. He seemed a little lost.

"No, please, come! It'll be fun," I said. I tried to sound convincing.

"Okay," Joey said, still hesitant.

I wondered if I wanted Joey to come along so I could be with him or deep down in the hope of making Billy jealous. Was it to show Billy that I had someone, too?

# CHAPTER 16

Before we left the theater, Savannah called Belinda's and asked if they could keep a late night table open for us. Belinda was more than happy to oblige since Savannah had held a number of parties there over the years.

We walked through the Quarter to Belinda's with Savannah chatting the whole way there. She loved showing off the Quarter to first-timers, and since Steve had never been there, she went on and on about some of the history. She pointed out things like the house Tennessee Williams was rumored to have spent many nights with his lover and the Mint bar, which also had female impersonators. She admitted the Mint was the only true competition for her own business.

Steve seemed very interested in everything she had to say. He would nod politely and ask a question every now and then.

"I wonder if Tennessee was a top or a bottom?" he asked her.

Savannah pondered the thought.

"Probably versatile," she answered.

I noticed how Billy stayed close by his side. Even their steps were at the same exact pace. Billy's eyes stayed on him most of the time. He grabbed onto Steve's arm at one point and leaned against him with a complete look of contentment.

I didn't say much the whole way. I was too busy observing Steve. I thought he seemed a little obnoxious, like when he slightly snorted while laughing at one of Savannah's jokes or when he rolled his eyes when some guy passing by checked him out.

Joey was walking a couple of steps behind me. I don't recall him saying one word the whole time. He looked pretty uncomfortable. I felt bad because I knew where my attention was going all of a sudden, but I felt like I couldn't help it.

At Belinda's, once we were at our table, Belinda served up hot cornbread muffins with a huge cup of sweet butter.

"Cornbread! Now that's something I haven't seen in a while!" Billy exclaimed. He immediately reached for one in the wicker basket that held the muffins.

"I can only imagine the calories!" Steve said in horror. "I'd have to do an extra fifty crunches if I ate that."

Billy had put the muffin on his bread plate, but he immediately seemed uninterested in it.

"Yeah, true. A lot of calories in that," Billy agreed.

Savannah sat at the head of the table, with Billy and Steve on one side and me and Joey on the other. Joey fiddled with his napkin. Under the table, I reached for his knee and squeezed it. His eyes met mine, and I smiled at him. He smiled back, but he still didn't seem too enthused.

"So you're an actor, Steve?" Savannah asked, while spreading extra butter on her cornbread.

"Yes, I'm here to perform a few shows of a new musical called *North Pacific*," he said, suspiciously eyeing the fried pickles Belinda brought out.

"The one playing at the Saenger?" Savannah asked.

"That's the one," Steve said, beaming widely.

"He got great reviews in New York," Billy piped in.

Steve smiled at the praise.

"How'd you two meet?" I found myself asking.

"I'd like to hear, also," Savannah said. She sipped her glass of wine.

"Well…" Billy started to say.

Steve reached over and patted Billy's hand as if to say, "I'll tell this story."

"I was a manager at the coffeehouse where Billy was working. I hired him in fact."

"Oh, really," Savannah said.

Billy looked down at the table. A look of embarrassment swept over his face. Joey began to fidget in his chair.

"I guess you can say it was love at first sight. He was so young and fresh. You don't find that often in New York."

"Fresh, yes," Savannah muttered.

"And we've been together ever since. Three glorious months," Steve said. He leaned over and placed a peck on Billy's cheap.

"You must have met right after Billy made it to New York," I said. I tried to figure out the timeline in my head.

"Pretty much right after he got off the bus," Steve said.

"That was quick," I said. My tone was slightly harsh, and that caught everyone's attention. I felt both Joey and Savannah's eyes on me.

"Divine intervention I guess," Steve said.

Billy smiled, a little too widely to be believed.

"And so what do you do, Larry?" Steve said to Joey.

"That's Joey," he replied.

"Oh, yes. Please forgive me. I'm a little fatigued after all of this travel," Steve said. He rubbed his temples dramatically.

"I work for Savannah, as her stage manager," Joey answered.

"Ah, yes. How charming that must be," Steve said. He gave that actor smile once again.

"He's just been a godsend to me," Savannah said.

She reached over and patted him on the back.

"And how long have the two of you been together?" Steve asked, looking straight at Joey and me.

I saw Billy looking at me out of the corner of my eye. That Billy Harris smile was nowhere to be seen.

I looked at Joey. I wasn't sure what to say. After all, did he consider us together?

"Uh…" I started to say.

Just then Belinda showed up with everyone's order, including a garden salad with oil and vinegar on the side for Steve.

And the topic was not brought up again.

Not too soon after dinner, Steve insisted that they had to go back to his hotel room. He just had to get some rest before rehearsals the next morning. Billy told me he would call me the next day, and we could hang out while Steve was at work.

They caught a cab right outside of Belinda's, as did Savannah who said she too was exhausted. Joey and I decided to walk back. The residential streets of the Quarter were pretty quiet on this Wednesday evening, except for the occasional drunk, lost tourist, or random person carrying their malt liquor in brown paper bags.

The whole night had seemed like one big dysfunctional tailspin. Joey was still quiet. I wasn't sure if he was upset that I never answered Steve's question about our relationship, or if it was that he sensed my feelings for Billy. Were they that obvious?

"That was him, wasn't it?" Joey asked, as we neared Savannah's.

"Who?" I said.

Joey sort of grunted and stuffed his hands in his pocket. He knew that I knew what he was talking about, and he wasn't up for playing games.

"The guy you told me about. The one from high school that you had a crush on."

I quickly debated in my head what to say. I then realized that there really wasn't any good way to say it. I did like Joey. I really did. I just don't think even I realized what an effect Billy still had on me. Billy hadn't been in town for more than three hours, and I already felt like that awkward sixteen-year old again who used to sit in his room with him late at night and hang on his every word.

"Yeah, but that was a long time ago," I finally said, trying to sound convincing.

"You barely took your eyes off of him the whole night," Joey said. He slowed his steps down and looked more at the sidewalk than at me.

What could I say? He was right. I knew it. He deserved better than that. He had been so amazing to me, and the minute Billy was in town I practically started to ignore him.

"I was just surprised to see him. That's all," I said, reaching out and taking his hand.

He looked up at me. Those eyes that I had always found so beautiful seemed so full of hurt, and I knew I was the one that had put that hurt there.

"I should probably get home," he said. He pulled his hand away. "Good night."

"Joey…" I called after him.

He turned back around one last time and said," 'Night, Mason."

I stood on the corner of the street and watched him walk down the street.

"Hey, can you tell me where the nearest tity bar is?" a drunk man in a business suit asked me as he staggered by.

"Sorry, no," I said.

The drunk guy noticed me staring at Joey walk down the street

"I guess you wouldn't know where the tity bars are, huh?" he laughed.

And then he continued staggering down the street.

The next morning I immediately tried to call Joey. He wasn't at home. I tried again a couple of hours later. I was convinced he was avoiding my calls.

*After all, in that kind of situation you always think that it's all about you.*

Later, I remembered that he said he had to go to the community college to register for classes.

Resigning myself to the fact that I wouldn't be able to speak to him yet, I prepared to deal with Billy. He called around noon the next day and asked if he could meet me at the Jax Brewery, a huge tourist oriented mall on Decatur that once was a beer brewery. He wanted to buy some New Orleans souvenirs for some new friends back in New York.

I met him at the front entrance, and he looked like he hadn't slept the whole night. His eyes were red with dark bags underneath them. His shirt was wrinkled, and he wore the same jeans from last night.

"Hey, Mace!" he said. He threw his arms around me and gave me a bear hug.

"Hey," I muttered.

For someone who professed to be so happy and in this great relationship, he sure looked like shit.

"Isn't it cool that I'm here and we get to spend the afternoon together?" he asked, while we walked into the mall.

"Yeah, cool," I said. "So how is New York? Really?"

"New York is cool. I kinda lucked out," he said. He stopped in front of a fudge store and practically drooled. "Fudge!"

"You never did tell me where you were staying," I said.

He hesitated.

"With Steve."

I knew I didn't know jack shit about relationships, but I did know three months was a little soon to move in together.

"Wow! Already?" I asked.

We went into some store that sold nothing but hats-crazy hats, ladies hats for formal occasions, and men's caps. He tried on a red beret and immediately put it back on the rack while shaking his head.

"Uh, yeah. When I met him, it turned out he was looking for a roommate."

"Don't you work for him?"

"I worked with him," Billy corrected. "Then I guess things just kind of progressed pretty quickly."

"Oh."

"He's a nice guy," Billy said, trying to convince me.

"What do you think I should get?" he asked.

We stopped in front of another tourist trap store that sold nothing but Mardi Gras beads next.

"I'm not sure," I said. "He seems a little...old for you."

Billy shrugged his shoulders.

"What is age really?" he asked. "Some predetermined societal categorization?"

*What?*

"It just seems a little..."

"Oh, what about these ones? With the little beer cans on them?" he said. He picked a pair of beads with small plastic Jax beer cans all around it. "This is so cool! The girl I work with will die. She's always wanted to come here ever since she saw some video with all of those chicks showing their boobs at Mardi Gras."

"Billy, can I ask you something?"

He sighed. He was smart enough to know I wasn't letting this go.

"Sure, Mace. Ask away. Whatever."

"I know your grand plan was always to go to New York and get the hell out of Andrew Springs, but are you happy there? I mean really?"

"Well, yeah. It's New York, Mace! It's like cooler than cool. The city that doesn't sleep and all that stuff, remember?"

He walked off towards the cashier and bought two pairs of the beer can beads.

When he walked back he said, "Let's get some food. My treat. I'm starved!"

"Okay," I said giving in. There was no way I was getting more information out of him.

"It really is great to see you again, Mace," he said. Much to my surprise, and to the little old cashier lady, he leaned over and placed a small kiss on my cheek. "It really is great."

# CHAPTER 17

When I got back to Aunt Savannah's, she was filing her nails and listening to some jazz. Wednesdays were usually a slow night so she often didn't leave until six.

"Hey," I said walking in.

She gave me a stern look that reminded me to take off my shoes before I walked on her new white carpet.

"Did you have fun with your friend?"

"Uh, yeah," I said.

Billy had headed back to the hotel to meet Steve for dinner.

"His boyfriend was quite interesting," she said, with a smirk.

I took off my shoes and left them next to the front door and started to head to the kitchen. I wasn't really in the mood to discuss the whole Billy situation.

"Yeah, I guess," I said.

"You seemed sort of quiet last night when we went to dinner. Both you and Joey barely said a word."

I noticed another huge bouquet of white and pink roses out on the balcony.

"More flowers from your admirer?" I asked smiling.

She waved her hand at me as if to disregard them.

"I suppose."

"And who is this mystery man?"

"Just an old friend from long ago. Don't try and change the subject on me, young man! I saw how you reacted towards Billy last night. I also noticed that Joey picked up on it, too."

I suspected that I wouldn't get out of this conversation so I sat down on the couch next to her. Maybe she would be able to help me with some guidance because I sure as hell didn't seem to know what I was doing.

"I guess I have some old feelings for Billy that kind of crept up when I saw him again," I admitted out loud finally.

"Um...hmmm...tell me something I don't know!"

"Was it really that obvious?"

"Maybe if someone was deaf and blind they wouldn't have picked up on it," she said. She scooted to the edge of the sofa and put her nail file down. "Listen to me, Little Bit. I don't know what's going on with your friend, Billy, but something about that whole relationship he has going on with that guy is a little fishy. What I do know is that Joey really likes you, and I haven't seen him open up this much to anyone since his mother died. Don't screw up anything you might be starting with Joey over some boy you used to have a crush on."

I nodded.

"You practically disregarded Joey as soon as you saw this Billy character again. All night long I don't think you took your eyes off of Billy for five seconds."

"I know," I said, my head hanging down. "Joey is a great guy, but I can't help these feelings that I have for Billy. They're feelings I've had for a long time."

She sighed and picked up her nail file again. I knew that as much as she cared about me that she also cared about Joey. She had become his surrogate mother, and she didn't want to see him get hurt, either.

"I don't want to let them get in the way with Joey. I don't!" I insisted.

*But did I believe it completely?*

"Well, then you need to go over to Joey's right now, and be straight up with him. Tell him that."

"I've been trying to call him all day."

"Well, then go and wait for him if he's not there. If you really want to let him know you care, you have to show him. You're young, and you may not think so now, but life's too short. Trust me."

I then looked back out at the flowers on the balcony. If she was completely uninterested in this guy, then why would she have bothered to put them in her favorite vase?

"So why aren't you pursuing this guy who obviously has the hots for you?"

She got up and brushed off her skirt.

"Trust me. Don't do as I do, but do as I say," she said, with a hint of sadness in her voice.

So I took her advice, and I made my way over to Joey's. The skies were beginning to darken and you could smell the rain in the air. The streets of the Quarter were beginning to empty as everyone sensed the impending storm. I had already seen that when it rained in New Orleans it rained hard, and the streets often began to flood when the drainage system could not keep up.

I tried to hurry because, of course, I had forgotten my umbrella. All I needed was to show up at his place soaking wet and with my wavy hair beginning to frizz as it often did in rainy weather.

By the time I made it to Joey's, the first drops were beginning to fall from the sky. I prayed he would be home. If not, I would be stuck outside, but I would do it. I wanted him to know I was serious.

I really was. *Really.*

I knocked on the door and hoped for the best.

No answer.

Of course.

So I sat on his step and hoped that the small awning above his door would protect me from the rain. Soon after, I saw Joey coming down the street. He slowed down a bit when he saw me as if to delay the inevitable, which hurt me.

I stood up and thanked God for small favors. I could get inside before my hair looked like I had taken a bath with my stereo in the water with me.

"Hey, Joey!" I said. I tried to sound chipper. "I've been trying to call you all day, but then I remembered that you were going to register for classes."

"Uh, yeah. I'm surprised to see you here. I thought you would be hanging out with your friend," he said. He tried to juggle the college catalogs while he fished for the keys in his pocket.

I grabbed the catalogs so he could get his keys out.

"I saw him earlier. I was hoping we could talk."

"Yeah, sure…"

At that point Miss Althea's door swung open, and she stepped out wearing a long black dress, black hat, and black gloves.

"Boy, I was wondering if you were going to show up," she said. "I was about to pull my weave out I was so nervous up in here."

I looked at Miss Althea, then at Joey, and then Miss Althea.

"I'm sorry. I got held up. I'll be ready in just a sec," Joey said.

"You're going somewhere?" I asked.

"You's damn right he is! He's going with me over to my ex-*huzzband's*. I've got some things to pick up, and a lady cannot show up for this kind of thing on her own."

"Huh?" I asked.

"Miss Althea," Miss Althea began, "had to break things off with her *huzzband*. Seems he was *a-shamed* of me when it came to meeting his family. I don't play that since I is what I is-the whole package."

She shocked me and grabbed her crotch revealing a large....well....

"Says his family is one of the oldest, and did I mention whitest, in New Orleans, and they wouldn't understand. Well, I'm too old to play that shit," she said. She motioned for Joey. "Come on. We gotta go-now!"

Joey looked up at me from the bottom of the steps. His eyes told me that deep down he would like to talk to me after all.

"I'm sorry," he said. "I promised her this morning."

"It's okay. I'll catch up with you tonight," I promised.

"Come on, baby!" Miss Althea said. She grabbed for his hand.

Joey sighed and took the college catalogs back from me and started to head down the street with Miss Althea, so that she could pick up whatever the hell it was at her *ex-huzzband's*.

So mission failed, I decided to head home, and then, of course, it started pouring down rain. Instead of running down the streets, I actually took my time. If I was going to get soaked, oh, well. What the hell did it matter?

By the time I made it back to Savannah's, I looked like a drowned rat, a drowned rat that had screwed up. I just wanted to go inside, take a hot shower, and maybe take a nap before I had to go to work.

I took my shoes off outside the front door. Savannah would really have a breakdown if I walked in with my shoes after a rainstorm.

"Don't worry! I'm taking my shoes off, Aunt Savannah!" I called out.

When I walked in, I heard a voice that made me stop in my tracks say, "She's not here."

I looked into the living room and saw, of all people, Mother.

"Mother," I stammered. "How'd you get here?"

She flashed me a look of surprise.

"In a car?" I asked.

"Yes, in a car," she said, rolling her eyes. "Let's go get some food. I'm starved."

She picked up an umbrella off the floor.

"And I have an umbrella."

With everything that happened over the past couple of days I thought I had been through enough of an emotional roller coaster.

*Guess not.*

So without questioning my mother, I went ahead and took a shower and changed into some dry clothes.

I couldn't have been more shocked if the Pope had been there and asked me to go to dinner.

We walked to a small Italian place around the corner from Savannah's and sat at a table by the window. The rain had begun to let up, but now the sky was darkening with night.

"I still can't believe you drove here," I said. I shook my head in amazement.

"Well, after your father's heart attack I guess I decided I knew what real fear felt like. Driving to New Orleans, that was nothing compared to sitting next to your father's hospital bed and wondering if he was going to live."

"How is he?"

"Good. Cherie is home watching him. I think he realized that if he didn't change his ways he might not see Lily grow up. So he decided to shape up. No more salt or butter for him."

My father not eating salty foods drenched in butter? I couldn't imagine.

We both ordered huge plates of meatballs and spaghetti with Barq's root beers in glass bottles, of course.

"Why are you here?" I finally asked.

She ran her fingers through her loose hair, (Wait, did she color it? The gray was gone.) and took a deep breath.

"Well, I hated the way we ended things the last time we saw each other."

Holy shit! She was apologizing? Who was this woman? When was her body taken over by alien beings with a twisted sense of humor?

"Yeah, it was kinda rough," I said.

*To say the least.*

"I'm not going to say I like your decision to move here. I'm not going to say I'm happy about your not going to college. I hate it."

I shifted uncomfortably in my seat. Did she drive all the way here just to give me a lecture?

"And?" I said.

"It's your life, Mason. You're an adult now. There may be a lot of things that I…don't understand. I may never. But you're going to do what you want to do, and you're still my son."

Was she actually referring to my being gay?

"I was very scared when you're dad was in the hospital. I've been with him since I was a teenager. I'm not sure if I would know how to go about things without him," she said quietly. "I said some things to you I shouldn't have said at the time. It certainly was not the place for it. Your attention should have been on your father and not on our arguing."

"I was scared, too, you know."

"I know, baby. I know," she said. She nodded her head. "So I was going to call you, but then I decided that I should tell you in person that I'm sorry."

I reached across the table and grabbed her hand.

"I'm glad you did," I said.

She drove back that night saying she wanted to get back to my father but not before giving me a new picture of Lily.

I felt like things would finally be okay with my mother.

I headed over to work. I was anxious to tell Joey that I was sorry. Sometimes, like my mom, we do things or say things that are just plain stupid. You just got to own up to them. Sure, I may have some old feelings for Billy in my heart. But that didn't mean that I wasn't open to letting in new feelings for Joey...

And to let them take over.

# CHAPTER 18

I made it to the theater and immediately saw Savannah. She was helping out at the box office because Beau was home with the flu. I could tell she was eager to find out how things went with my mother.

"Well?" she asked eagerly.

"Things are cool with me and Mother, if that's what you mean."

"Well, yes, that's what I mean," she said relieved.

"Where's Joey?" I asked.

"He told me you had stopped by to talk to him, but he had to leave."

"I just want to make things right with him, too," I said. I looked at the long line of people outside the window.

"Go ahead," she said, waving me off. "I can handle this for a while longer."

"Thank you," I said.

I gave her a quick peck on the cheek.

"The things I do for love," I heard her mutter as I left.

I went backstage and asked one of the drag queens where Joey was. She told me to look near the stage.

Sure enough, there he was fiddling with the lights for the night.

"How did things go with Miss Althea's husband, I mean *ex-huzzband*?"

He smiled.

"He wasn't home. So she took her stuff and wrote him a nasty note with her lipstick on his bathroom mirror."

"I'm sorry we didn't get to talk," I said.

I heard the crowd getting restless in their seats. The show would be starting soon.

"After the show why don't you come by my place?" he offered.

"I'll be there!" I said.

I went up to him and gave him a quick kiss, which seemed to please him. I hoped that we could just go back to the way things were before Billy showed back up and sent my emotions into a tailspin. I then went to the box office to wrap things up for Savannah. She would have to start the show soon.

Right after the show I went backstage to meet up with Joey so that we could head over to his place to talk.

"Hi," I said, greeting him with a kiss. "Are you ready to take off?"

"I think I pretty much have everything wrapped up here," he said. He looked much happier.

Savannah walked backstage carrying a bottle of water in one hand and her high heels in the other.

"We've got a problem, Little Bit. The receipts for tonight aren't balancing, and with Beau not here I'm totally lost."

Of all nights! They had balanced every freaking night before this one. This meant I would have to go through every transaction of the night.

"Okay, I'll be right there," I said.

Savannah then left to take care of a customer that was still arguing about their drink check with the bartender. It was a crazy night.

"I'll wait for you," Joey offered.

I knew it would probably take me a while. Chances are it would not be a quick process.

Even though I hated to say it, I said," There's no point in you waiting here. Why don't you go on home, and when I'm done I'll come over."

"That's okay. I can wait."

I could look in his eyes and tell he was exhausted though.

"Go home and take a shower. Relax. As soon as I'm done I'll be right over."

"Are you sure?"

"Yes," I answered.

I placed another little kiss on his lips.

After an hour of going through every transaction of the nigh, I found the one that I missed. I was usually great with numbers, but I guess my mind was all over the place that night.

I walked into the bar area and found Savannah sipping on a glass of wine with Ernie, the bartender.

"Found it," I said.

"Good job," she said. "Now go take of things with Joey."

She winked at me.

"I will," I said.

When I walked out into the lobby on my way to Joey's, I was startled to find Billy. He looked lost and disoriented. His eyes were red from crying.

"Billy!"

"Mason!" he said.

He threw his arms around me and sobbed.

# CHAPTER 19

I sat Billy on the sofa in the lobby and went into the bar to get him a soda. Savannah looked surprised to see me when I walked back in. She poured another glass for Ernie and herself.

"Young man, weren't you on your way to Joey's?" she asked.

"I was, but Billy just showed up. He's upset about something. I haven't been able to get it out of him yet."

She sighed.

"Well, you better not keep Joey waiting too long," she said.

"I'm not, but what can I do?"

She sighed again, as if to say she could tell me what I should do. I began to think that she wasn't one of Billy's greatest fans.

When I walked back into the lobby, Billy was wiping another tear away. He looked so vulnerable and even innocent.

"What is it? What happened?" I asked.

I sat next to him and handed him a cola.

"It's over!" he said.

"Over?"

"Me and Steve. Finished. Done."

I didn't know what to say. I'm happy! He was too old for you! The situation seemed weird! None of it seemed right at the time, even if I was thinking it in my head.

"What happened?"

"He told me to come to the show tonight. But I told him I already had seen the show-a lot! I wanted to just hang out tonight in the Quarter while I could.

He went on and on about how I didn't care about him, about how ungrateful I was, and how I was just staying with him for the money."

*Well, was he?*

"What did you tell him?"

"I told him it wasn't true! That's not how I feel," he said.

He sounded like he was trying to convince himself of it.

I didn't say anything.

"Well, it's not!" he yelled.

"I didn't say it was, Billy," I replied.

I tried to choose my words carefully.

"It just seems like your relationship happened really fast, and he is a lot older than you."

"So you're happy it's over!" he said accusingly.

"No. Don't be crazy. Billy, I care about you. I hate to see you this upset," I said. I felt my own eyes tearing up.

He calmed down, took a deep breath, and then looked into my eyes.

"You do, don't you?"

"I think you know how much I care about you," I said, looking away.

I felt my heartbeat quicken.

"Yeah, I do know. You've always been there for me. No matter what," he said.

I felt his hand glide over my knee and rest over my own hand.

As always, his touch seemed to send an electrical pulse straight through my body.

"Billy, I…"

"Remember that Christmas Eve night?" he asked.

"You remember it?" I asked, astonished that he had brought it up.

"Of course. How could I not? I wasn't that drunk," he laughed.

I was totally taken aback.

"You never mentioned it though."

"I guess there were just a lot of things I wasn't ready to deal with at the time. My big focus was to leave Andrew Springs and get the hell of there," he paused. "What do I do now, Mace? What do I do?"

"It'll work out. Somehow."

I felt his hand squeeze mine, and the next thing I knew he leaned over and started kissing me. Right there and then! He wrapped his arms around me and pulled me close to him. My mind, of course, drifted back to that night…which in some ways seemed so long ago.

In the background, I heard a door slam. Startled, both of us jumped, but there was no one in the lobby.

I looked out the front window, and I saw of all people Joey. He must've seen Billy and me kissing.

"Oh, shit!' I said, standing up.

"What is it?" a bewildered Billy asked.

"I'll be back," I said.

I went running out the building after Joey. Once again, sprinkles of rain were beginning to fall. Another storm was on its way. You could feel it in the air.

"Joey!" I called after him.

He kept walking and did not look back.

Christ! What was he doing back at the theater? Why didn't he just stay at home?

I don't know if I had ever felt so guilty about something I had done. I felt like a piece of dog shit found on the bottom of your shoe.

I could tell he picked up his pace, so I continued to run after him. When I finally caught him, he was standing on the corner of Dauphine Street.

"Joey!" I said. I grabbed his arm and made him stop.

He turned around, but he refused to look me in the eye.

"Joey, it's not...it's just..."

"I decided I would come back and meet you so you wouldn't have to walk by yourself," he said softly.

"I'm sorry you saw that," I said.

"I'm not," he said. He shook his head. "I needed to see it. You've still got it bad for that guy. Just admit it, Mason. It's obvious."

I was silent. I didn't know what to say I felt so confused inside.

"See. Deep down I could sense it," he said. "Couldn't you have just been honest with me? With yourself?"

"I'm sorry," I said desperately.

Whereas Billy was a master at always seeming to jerk me around, Joey had never been that way. Of course, this was the thanks that he got.

"It was really hard for me you know..." he started to say.

"Hard for what?'

"I had cut out so many people after my mom died-friends, other family. She was the person I could always count on, and then you came along."

Thunder roared in the background.

"You seemed so sweet and innocent. I started to let myself have fun again. But, I can't do this, Mason, when you've still got a thing for this other guy."

He started to walk off, and I grabbed for him again. He shook me off and nodded his head no.

"I don't want to talk about this anymore right now. I need some time to myself," he said.

Yet again, I watched him walk away as the rain began to pour.

I slowly walked back to the theater as everything I had done was beginning to sink in. Sure, Billy started the kiss, but I certainly had not pushed him away.

Billy was still sitting on the sofa. He seemed in disbelief that I had gotten up and left him.

"I was wondering if you were coming back," he said.

"Sorry, I had to take care of something. Or try and take care of it."

I sat down next to him, and he started to place his hand on my knee.

"Do you think it'll be okay if I crash at your aunt's tonight? I can't go back to the fucking hotel room where Steve is."

"Yeah, I'm sure it won't be a problem."

Savannah looked at me disapprovingly as I took extra linens out of the bedroom closet to give to Billy, who was sleeping on the couch. He said he just wanted to crash. He couldn't think about anything else that night.

She was wearing one of the long, flowing silk nightgowns she seemed so fond of, her arms crossed and shaking her head.

"What?" I asked, even though I knew what she was thinking.

"Did you go and talk to Joey?"

I still had not told her what had happened.

"We talked," I said. I reached for another pillow at the top of the closet.

"Yeah, well, if Billy has truly ended it with this Steve, then how is he getting back to New York? Is he going back?"

That was something I was wondering myself. Once again, I was left trying to read between the lines and figure out what Billy's kiss meant.

"I don't know," I answered.

"Huh," she said, under her breath.

Of course, she thought I had screwed things up with Joey, and of course I had.

As I walked down the hall to the living room, I decided I would ask Billy exactly what his plans were, what had his kiss meant, and where do we go from here.

I was greeted by that sound that took me back yet again a couple of years. *Snoring!*

Billy fell asleep right before I could ask him all of these questions. And just as I had that night, I covered him up with a quilt and headed off to bed myself. One more time, he left me hanging.

When I got up the next morning and walked to the bathroom, I heard rustling around going on in the living room. It was much too early for Savannah to get up from bed. It was seven o'clock in the morning. So I knew it had to be Billy.

I walked into the living room, and he had already folded up all of the linens left them in a neat pile on the edge of the couch.

"You're up already?" I asked, running my fingers through my frizzy bed head hair.

"Morning, Mace," he said, all lively and full of spirit.

"I can't believe you're up already," I repeated.

Like Savannah, Billy was never one to actually see the sun rise.

"Guess what happened?" he asked excitedly. He clasped his hands together as if in prayer.

"What?"

I stumbled towards the couch and wiped the sleep out of my eyes.

"I just got off the phone with Steve," he said.

"You did?"

"It's so great! We made up! Everything can go back to normal!"

"Whoa! Wait!" I said, not sure I had heard him right. "I thought you guys had such a big blow up last night that it was completely over. And you kissed…"

"Mace, I'm learning that things happen in relationships. People have conflict. You have to work through them. It's the adult thing to do."

He began putting on his shoes.

"We leave for New York this afternoon," he said, matter of factly, while putting double knots in his shoelaces as always. Better to do that than to risk them coming undone and falling flat on your face, he used to say.

"But, Billy, this makes no freaking sense!" I protested.

"I guess sometimes love doesn't," he said, with a far off look on his face. "And besides I have to get back to New York. There's so much there I still haven't seen or had the chance to do."

He stood up, walked over, and gave me a hug.

"You should come and visit me and Steve as soon as you get a chance," he said, as he pulled away. "I'm glad we got to hang out again."

"Uh, yeah, whatever," I mumbled.

Now, okay, I admit it. I was pissed. After everything I did for him the previous night, he was running right back to this guy.

He started heading towards the door where the bright morning sun shined through the window. The rain had completely cleared up. I could see the sky outside was clear now.

"You know, Mace," he said. He turned around and looked at me. "You're a really great guy and a good friend. You deserve to have someone special in your life, someone who knows how to treat you well. That Joey guy seemed kinda nice."

And with that he walked out the door.

I sat in my pajamas on the sofa and just stared at the television. The newscaster, Angela Hill, was on the channel four morning news talking about the tornadoes that the storm had produced last night. Of course, one had ripped through some houses on Grand Isle, a below sea level area of coastal homes not far from New Orleans. Those people were always being flooded out of their homes. Every time a hurricane, a tropical storm, or hell, even a hard rain came along that place got flooded faster than a televangelist could condemn gay people. You would have thought that they would have learned by the second, third, or umpteenth time. But later the news would show them moving back into the homes they had just evacuated again.

"I just love it here! I couldn't imagine being anywhere else," a woman, missing all her bottom front teeth told a reporter in one broadcast.

I just didn't understand it.

Finally, I realized I had to snap out of it. I had done what I had done. There was no going back into the past. I had hurt Joey. Bad. I had jerked him around. For what?

The people in Grand Isle didn't seem surprised when it flooded. Why was I when it came to Billy's actions? Why was I when he sent me mixed signals-again?

All I could do was go to Joey and beg for a second chance. To hope that maybe he could let us start over-start over from a point where I had begun to let go of those feelings I had for Billy Harris-the feelings that I finally had to completely admit to myself would never be returned from him, at least not the way that I wanted.

So I jumped up, took a shower, and got dressed.

I knew what I had to do.

The heat was on. Even though October would be here soon, it felt like it was the first of August. At nine o'clock in the morning, it was well past ninety degrees.

On the walk to Joey's, I began to sweat profusely under my arms, and I realized that in my rush I had forgotten to put on deodorant. I contemplated turning back and going home to do so, but I decided that this was too important. I had to talk to Joey.

With my guilt eating away at me, I stopped at the A & P and bought a bouquet of flowers. After all, isn't that what one did in these types of situations- show up with flowers? Don't they help ease the pain of asking for forgiveness?

"Oh, baby, them flowers sho' was pretty, too. Um, um, um," Miss Althea said. She shook her head and looked at the wilting flowers on the step next to me in front of Joey's. "I'll put' em in some water. Maybe they can still be saved."

She put down her grocery bags from Schwegmann's and scooped up the flowers.

"Cheer up, baby. I'm sure that boy will be back sometime soon," she said, opening up her apartment.

She stopped, and then tilted her head as if she were in deep thought.

"Although Shreveport sho' is a long ways from here. And he did seem kinda upset when he left, too. You two have some sort of a fight or something?"

"I guess you could say that," I said. I really did not want to get into it with her.

She took her groceries in one bag at a time, and before she shut the door she said, "It'll be okay, baby. I'm sho' ya'll work it out, and thanks for them pretty flowers. They'll real look nice on Miss Althea's kitchen table."

She shut the door leaving me sitting on the step.

Joey had left that morning for his aunt's, and he didn't say when he would be back. He just upped and left, and I knew I was the cause of it.

When I made it back to Savannah's, she was finally up. She was making coffee and biscuits, despite the fact that it wasn't even Saturday.

She gave me a knowing look when I walked in.

I sat at the table and poured myself a cup of coffee.

"Joey left town, didn't he?"

"You know?" I muttered.

"He left me a message on my machine saying he needed a few days off for personal reasons, and he hoped that I understood," she said.

"Yeah, Miss Althea told me he had left when I went over."

I sipped my coffee-black. No point in adding sugar.

"Billy's gone, too," she commented.

"Went back to Steve," I mumbled.

"Hmmmm," she said, taking biscuits out of the oven.

"I fucked up, Aunt Savannah," I said.

She put the pan of biscuits on the stove, walked over, and patted me on the head.

"Well, Little Bit, we all do sometimes," she said. "It's what we do afterwards that counts."

"And what do you think I should do?" I asked. I desperately hoped she would have some sort of wise advice that would make all of this mess clear up.

"What do you think?" she asked.

She sat across from me and sipped her own coffee.

"I wish I could tell Joey that I realized what a jackass I was. I wish I could tell him that I think he's a wonderful guy, and that I wish I had another chance with him. I want a chance to show him how special he is to me."

"Then why don't you do that?" she asked.

"Because he's left for Shreveport!" I exclaimed.

I thought I had stated the obvious.

"Well, no one's saying you can't go after him."

"Do what?" I said, feeling helpless. "I don't even know where he would be there."

"Well, I know his aunt owns a place called Lucy's Diner. If you went there and found it, I'm sure you could track him down. If you *try* hard enough."

I realized she was right. If I truly felt as passionately about this as I said I did, I would do it. Nothing could stop me.

"But how am I going to even get there?" I asked, coming up with one more obstacle.

Savannah reached over to the counter behind her, picked up her car keys, and tossed them to me. I caught them in mid-air despite never being able to catch a football for my father.

"Take the convertible?" I asked.

"Well, it's the fastest way you'll get there. There's a map of the state of Louisiana under the front passenger seat. It'll show you how to get there. It'll lead your way."

"You don't mind?"

"I'm giving you the means, Little Bit. Don't let yourself and Joey down. You should at least give it a shot. Give it all you have if it's what you really want."

"I do!" I said.

I stood up and felt energized all of a sudden.

*I had to do it. This was my chance!*

"Then hop to it," she said smiling. "Good luck."

"Thank you, Aunt Savannah!" I said.

I threw my arms around her and gave her a tight hug.

"Just don't total the car, okay?" she said, winking at me.

I started to turn around and take off.

"Oh, and you know what?" she said.

"What?"

"I've decided to take some of my own advice for a change and give that friend of mine a chance. There's gotta be some sort of romance left in the old girl."

"There's gotta be!" I said.

So now I'm headed down the interstate in my aunt's convertible. The top is down, and the wind is blowing my hair into one big frizzy mess. I don't care though. The rushing wind makes the suppressing heat seem not that bad anymore. It actually feels pretty damn freeing.

On the seat next to me is the map of Louisiana. I got a little lost, but I think I'm headed in the right direction now.

I hope I don't wreck Savannah's car, but somehow I think that even if I do get in a little fender bender, it certainly won't be the end of the world.

I'm not sure what Joey's reaction will be when he sees me pop up in Shreveport. Maybe he'll put his arms around me and kiss me like he did the first time. Maybe he'll slap me and tell me to go to hell. Either way, if I didn't go, I'd always wonder what would have happened if I had. I would have wondered if I could have won him back.

And isn't that half the battle of life? To take a chance and find out?

*Wish me luck!*

0-595-33756-2